The Great Gatsby

原著 └→ F. Scott Fitzgerald
改寫 └→ David A. Hill
譯者 └→ 安卡斯

大亨小傳

ABOUT THIS BOOK

For the Student

 Listen to the story and do some activities on your Audio CD.

 Talk about the story.

For the Teacher

Go to our Readers Resource site for information on using readers and downloadable Resource Sheets, photocopiable Worksheets, and Tapescripts. www.helblingreaders.com

For lots of great ideas on using Graded Readers consult Reading Matters, the Teacher's Guide to using Helbling Readers.

Structures

Modal verb would	Non-defining relative clauses
I'd love to . . .	Present perfect continuous
Future continuous	Used to / would
Present perfect future	Used to / used to doing
Reported speech / verbs / questions	Second conditional
Past perfect	Expressing wishes and regrets
Defining relative clauses	

Structures from other levels are also included.

CONTENTS

Francis Scott Key Fitzgerald was born in St. Paul, Minnesota, USA in 1896. His family were upper-middle class Irish Catholics. In 1913 he enrolled[1] at Princeton, a prestigious[2] university. While he was at university, he wrote his first novel. But it was rejected[3] by publishers. Five years later he left university without graduating and joined the army.

In 1919, he met and fell in love with Zelda Sayre. She was 17 and very beautiful. Fitzgerald wanted to marry her but she was only interested in money and having a good time[4]. To please her, he left the army and moved to New York to look for a job.

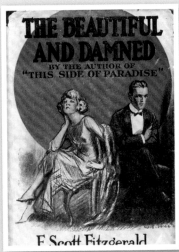

With the publication in March 1920 of his novel *This Side of Paradise*, Fitzgerald became a literary sensation[5]. He was now earning enough money to convince Zelda to marry him. They immediately embarked on[6] an extravagant lifestyle of parties and socializing, travelling widely both in the USA and in Europe.

His second novel *The Beautiful and Damned* (1922) and the third *The Great Gatsby* (1925) didn't sell as well as the first and he was frequently in debt[7]. In 1930, Zelda developed schizophrenia. From 1932 onwards she lived in mental institutions and she was a constant expense for Fitzgerald.

In 1937 Fitzgerald went to Hollywood and began working as a scriptwriter. He was drinking heavily and his health got steadily[8] worse. Eventually in 1940, he died of a heart attack.

1 enroll [ɪnˋrol] (v.) 入學註冊
2 prestigious [prɛsˋtɪdʒɪəs] (a.) 有聲望的
3 reject [rɪˋdʒɛkt] (v.) 拒絕;駁回
4 have a good time 盡興地玩樂
5 sensation [sɛnˋseʃən] (n.) 轟動之事物(在此指文壇新星)
6 embark on 著手進行
7 in debt 負債
8 steadily [ˋstɛdəlɪ] (adv.) 穩定地;持續地

Many of the events from Fitzgerald's early life appear in his most famous novel, *The Great Gatsby*. It was his third novel and it was published in 1925, right in the middle of the period known as The Jazz Age. It has been called the first 'modern' American novel because it describes the new society after World War I and before the Wall Street Crash[1] and the depression of the 1930s. It is a love story but it is also about the end of the American Dream.

The story is set on the East coast, in New York, but the main characters in the story, Jay Gatsby, Nick Carraway, Tom and Daisy Buchanan, and Jordan Baker, all come from the Midwest – a rural, provincial part of America.

1 Wall Street Crash 指 1929 年的華爾街股災
2 self-made man 白手起家的人
3 decay [dɪˋke] (n.) 敗壞

Gatsby represents the newly rich of the USA. He is a self-made man[2], although the story suggests that he probably made his money by doing illegal business. Tom Buchanan represents the American aristocracy – families with old wealth. Both men live a life of leisure and luxury. They drive fast cars, travel a lot and have magnificent houses and expensive clothes.

Nick, the narrator, does not belong in the social world of Tom and Gatsby. He is only part of it by chance because he is Gatsby's neighbor and a cousin of Tom's wife, Daisy. At first he is fascinated by their world but in the end he feels disgust for the people surrounding Gatsby's life and for the emptiness and moral decay[3] of life among the wealthy on the East Coast. He decides to move back to the Midwest.

There are several films of *The Great Gatsby*. The most famous film is the 1974 version, starring Robert Redford and Mia Farrow.

1 Work with a partner. Look at this scene from *The Great Gatsby*. Make a list of the key words that you could use to describe it.

2 Write a paragraph with your partner to describe the picture. Use the key words in your list. Compare your description with those of other pairs in the class.

3 Look at the picture again. Would you like to be there? Why/why not? Explain your ideas to a partner.

4 Read the things that different people say about Jay Gatsby's past. Remember the story takes place in 1922, and World War I was 1914-18.

- ⓐ 'They say he's one of Kaiser Wilhelm's nephews. That's where all his money comes from.'
- ⓑ 'Somebody told me he had killed a man once.'
- ⓒ 'He was a German spy during the war.'
- ⓓ 'He was in the American army during the war.'
- ⓔ 'He told me once he was an Oxford man . . . however I don't believe him.'
- ⓕ 'A handsome man, and a perfect gentleman, isn't he? He went to Oxford College in England. It's one of the most famous colleges in the world.'
- ⓖ 'Young men didn't arrive from nowhere to buy a palace on Long Island Sound.'
- ⓗ 'He owned a lot of drugstores.'

Do you think it is possible that *all* these things are true? Why/why not? What does it tell you about Gatsby that people have such different ideas about his past? Discuss your ideas with a partner.

5 Look at these pictures of the main characters from the story. Write a few sentences to describe each of them. What do you think each person is like?

      Jay Gatsby   Daisy Buchanan   Tom Buchanan   Nick Carraway

6 Work with a partner. Compare your descriptions of the four characters.

7 These occupations and roles are mentioned in the story: Match them with the definitions (1-6).

1. a person who drives a car for other people
2. a person who cooks and cleans in someone's house
3. the most important male servant who looks after the house owner
4. an officer in the army
5. someone who makes their money by betting on things like horses or cards
6. a person who makes and sells something illegally, especially music or alcohol

_____ a. butler
_____ b. gambler
_____ c. lieutenant
_____ d. chauffeur
_____ e. bootlegger
_____ f. housekeeper

8 Sort the words in the box into groups. Each group must have at least 3 words in it. Give titles to the groups.

apartment   drive   front door   garage   gate   hall   jail
kitchen   lawn   mansion   music room   palace   path   porch
restaurant   station   steps   terrace   upstairs   verandah

9 Look at the pictures and label them with four words from Exercise **8**.

ⓐ _____

ⓑ _____

ⓒ _____

ⓓ _____

10 Complete the sentences with the words in Exercise **9**. Use each word once.

ⓐ A man arrived at eleven o'clock to cut the grass in my garden (Gatsby's _____ was always perfect).

ⓑ There was a wide _____ running along two sides of the Buchanan's house.

ⓒ Gatsby's yellow car was parked in the _____.

ⓓ Nick walked away from Gatsby's house and waited for his taxi near the _____.

1 run [rʌn] (v.) 經營
2 hardware [ˋhɑrd͵wɛr] (n.) 五金器具
3 graduate [ˋɡrædʒʊ͵et] (v.) 畢業
4 rent [rɛnt] (v.) 租
5 sound [saʊnd] (n.) 海峽
6 grand [ɡrænd] (a.) 雄偉的
7 second cousin 遠房的兄弟姊妹
8 drift [drɪft] (v.) 漂流；漂蕩

CHAPTER ONE

The Carraways have been a respected family for three generations in the Midwestern city where we live. My father runs[1] a hardware[2] business that has been in the family since 1851.

I graduated[3] from Yale University in 1915, and then fought in World War I. After that I decided to go to New York to work in the finance business. It was 1922.

I rented[4] a small, ugly house on Long Island. It was on one of a pair of large egg-shaped pieces of land that faced Long Island Sound[5]. My house was at the end of West Egg, the less fashionable of the two 'eggs', and only 50 meters from the sea. It was between two huge houses that were rented for fifteen thousand dollars a year. The one on my right was especially grand[6] and had 40 acres of garden. A gentleman called Gatsby lived there.

The story of the summer really begins on the evening I went to have dinner with the Buchanans. Daisy was my second cousin[7], and I'd known Tom at university. He was an athletic type and had played in the football team at Yale. His family was extremely rich. The couple had spent a year in France, and then had drifted[8] here and there, always mixing with rich people. This was a permanent move, Daisy said to me on the telephone, but I didn't believe her. Tom wasn't the kind of person to stay in one place for very long.

Anyway I drove to East Egg to see two people that I didn't really know very well. Their house was grander than I imagined – a red and white mansion[1] with a lawn[2] that stretched all the way down to the beach.

Tom had changed since I last saw him. He looked hard and arrogant now. The body under his riding clothes was muscular and powerful. It was a body that could hurt people, I thought.

We talked for a while on the porch[3] and then we went inside. Two young women were sitting on a couch[4]. I didn't recognize the younger one but Daisy got up and came over to greet me. She held my hand and looked into my face.

'I'm so happy to see you,' she said.

She told me that the other girl's surname was Baker and that she was staying with them. Daisy's face was sad and lovely, with bright eyes and a passionate mouth.

'You must see the baby,' she said.

'I'd like to.'

'She's asleep. She's three years old.'

'What do you do, Nick?' asked Tom.

'I'm in finance.'

'Which bank?'

I told him.

'Never heard of it,' he remarked[5].

'You will,' I answered. 'If you stay in the East.'

'Oh, I'll stay in the East,' he said looking at Daisy. 'I'd be a fool[6] to live anywhere else.'

---

1 mansion [ˈmænʃən] (n.) 大廈；宅第
2 lawn [lɔn] (n.) 草坪；草地
3 porch [portʃ] (n.) 門廊；入口處
4 couch [kautʃ] (n.) 長沙發
5 remark [rɪˈmɑrk] (v.) 談論；議論
6 fool [ful] (n.) 傻瓜

At this point Miss Baker said, 'Absolutely!'

It was the first word she had said since I came into the room. I looked at her. She was very slim[7] and she stood very straight. Her grey eyes looked out of a pale, charming, discontented face. I thought that I had seen her somewhere before.

'You live in West Egg, don't you?' she said. 'I know somebody there.'

'Really? I don't know anybody.'

'You must know Gatsby.'

'Gatsby?' demanded Daisy. 'Who's Gatsby?'

Before I could reply that he was my neighbor, dinner was announced and we moved onto the porch.

During dinner, Daisy and Miss Baker talked in a way that was as cool as their summer dresses.

'You make me feel uncivilized, Daisy,' I confessed later. 'Can't you talk about crops[8] or something?'

Suddenly the phone rang and the butler[9] went to answer it. He returned a minute later and whispered something in Tom's ear. Tom frowned[10] and, without a word, went inside. Daisy threw her napkin[11] on the table and followed him into the house.

I was about to speak when Miss Baker said 'Sh!'

Quiet but passionate speech could be heard from the next room. Miss Baker leaned[12] forward trying to hear.

'This Mr Gatsby you spoke about is my neighbor . . .,' I began.

'Don't talk. I want to hear what happens.'

'Is something happening?' I inquired[13] innocently.

---

7 slim [slɪm] (a.) 苗條的
8 crops [krɑps] (n.) (作複數形) 作物
9 butler [ˋbʌtlɚ] (n.) 男管家
10 frown [fraʊn] (v.) 皺眉；蹙額
11 napkin [ˋnæpkɪn] (n.) 餐巾
12 lean [lin] (v.) 傾斜
13 inquire [ɪnˋkwaɪr] (v.) 詢問

'Don't you know?' said Miss Baker, surprised. 'Tom's got a woman in New York.'

'Got a woman?' I repeated.

'It's really very insensitive of her to phone him at dinnertime!'

Almost before I really understood what she was saying, Tom and Daisy were back at the table.

After dinner, Miss Baker and Tom went into the library, and I followed Daisy onto the porch. We sat down side by side and talked for a while[1] about her daughter.

Then she said, 'We don't know each other very well, Nick, even if we are cousins. Well, I've had a very bad time. Everything's terrible. Everybody thinks so, and I *know*. I've been everywhere and seen everything and done everything.'

Her eyes were shining with emotion.

'I've become so sophisticated,' she said and laughed bitterly[2].

I wasn't convinced by her words. She wasn't being sincere. I felt uneasy[3].

We went to join Tom and Miss Baker in the library but when we got there, Miss Baker stood up and said: 'Ten o'clock. Time to go to bed.'

'Jordan's playing in a golf tournament[4] tomorrow,' explained Daisy.

'Oh – you're Jordan Baker,' I said.

I knew now why her face was familiar.

'Good night,' she said. 'Wake me at eight, please? Good night, Mr Carraway. See you soon.'

'Of course you will,' confirmed[5] Daisy. 'Come over often, Nick. I want you and Jordan to get to know each other.'

1 for a while 一會兒
2 bitterly [`bɪtəlɪ] (adv.) 苦澀地
3 uneasy [ʌnˋizɪ] (a.) 不自在的
4 tournament [ˋtɝnəmənt] (n.) 比賽；錦標賽
5 confirm [kənˋfɝm] (v.) 確認

After she'd left, Tom said, 'She's a nice girl.'

'Is she from New York?' I asked.

'From Louisville. We grew up there together,' said Daisy.

'Did you and Nick have a heart-to-heart talk[1] on the porch?' Tom asked her suddenly.

'Did we?' Daisy said. 'I don't remember.'

'Don't believe everything you hear, Nick,' he advised me.

As I was leaving, Daisy said, 'Oh, Nick! I forgot to ask you something important. We heard you were engaged[2] to a girl out West.'

'I'm too poor to think about marriage,' I replied.

I knew what she was talking about. There had been rumors[3] of marriage but this kind of gossip was one of the reasons I'd come East.

I was confused and a little disgusted as I drove away. I thought that Daisy should leave the house and take her baby with her – but she seemed to have no intention of doing that. As for Tom, I wasn't very surprised that he 'had a woman in New York'.

TOM BUCHANAN

* Nick says that Tom 'looked hard and arrogant'.
* Is there anything in Tom's behavior that shows Nick is right to think this?

1 heart-to-heart talk 嚴肅而坦率地談論私事；真心話
2 engage [ɪnˋgedʒ] (v.) 訂婚
3 rumor [ˋrumɚ] (n.) 謠言；傳聞
4 dock [dɑk] (n.) 碼頭；港區

It was a beautiful summer night, and I sat in my garden when I got home. Something in the distance moved and I realized that I wasn't alone. My neighbor was in his garden too. He was standing with his arms stretching out towards the water. I looked out to sea but I could only see a small green light. Perhaps it was the end of a dock[4]. When I looked back, Mr Gatsby had vanished, and I was alone again in the darkness.

CHAPTER TWO

I went to New York with Tom by train one Sunday afternoon. When it stopped at a drawbridge[1] to let boats through, Tom suddenly jumped up.

'Come on!' he said. 'I want you to meet my girl.'

We jumped off the train and walked back 100 meters to a small block[2] of buildings. It contained three shops, one of which was a garage. Tom went inside and I followed behind. The place was poor and bare[3]. A pale, blond man appeared.

'Hello, Wilson,' said Tom. 'How's business?'

'Can't complain,' answered Wilson. 'When are you going to sell me that car?'

'Next week. My man's working on it now.'

A woman in her mid-thirties appeared. She wasn't beautiful and she was a little plump[4] but there was life and energy in her body. She smiled slowly as she walked past her husband towards Tom. They shook hands, looking each other in the eyes.

'Get some chairs so we can sit down,' she said to her husband, without turning around.

'Sure.'

He went towards the office. His wife moved closer to Tom.

'I want to see you,' said Tom softly. 'Get on the next train.'

She nodded[5] and moved away from him just as Wilson brought in two chairs.

---

1 drawbridge [ˈdrɔ͵brɪdʒ] (n.)（可開閉的）吊橋
2 block [blɑk] (n.) 街區
3 bare [bɛr] (a.) 無設備的；空的
4 plump [plʌmp] (a.) 豐滿的
5 nod [nɑd] (v.) 點頭表示

Later we waited for her down the road and out of sight.

'Terrible place, isn't it?' said Tom.

'Awful.'

'It does her good to get away.'

'Doesn't her husband object[1]?'

'Wilson? He thinks she goes to see her sister. He's dumb[2].'

So Tom Buchanan, his girl and I went to New York. We took a cab[3] at the station.

At Fifth Avenue I said, 'I have to leave you here.'

'No,' said Tom. 'Myrtle will be hurt if you don't come to the apartment, won't you, Myrtle?'

'Come on,' she insisted. 'I'll telephone my sister Catherine. People say she's beautiful.'

The cab stopped in 158th Street.

'I'm going to invite the McKees, too,' Myrtle announced.

Myrtle's sister Catherine was a slim girl of thirty with red hair and a pale face. Mr McKee was a pale, feminine man from the flat below. He was a photographer. His wife was horrible. She told me proudly that her husband had photographed her a hundred and twenty-seven times.

Catherine sat down next to me and asked, 'Do you live on Long Island?'

'In West Egg.'

'I was there at a party a month ago. At a house that belongs to a man named Gatsby. Do you know him?'

'I live next door to him.'

'They say he's one of Kaiser Wilhelm's nephews. That's where all his money comes from.'

'I'd like to take some photos on Long Island,' McKee said. 'But I need a contact there.'

'Ask Myrtle,' said Tom and laughed.

At that moment, Mrs Wilson came in with a tray. 'Myrtle, give McKee a letter of introduction to your husband so he can do some studies of him.'

Catherine whispered to me. 'They both hate the person they're married to. I think they should get a divorce[4] and marry each other.'

I looked at her in surprise.

'It's Tom's wife that's keeping them apart,' she went on. 'She's a Catholic and she doesn't believe in divorce.'

Daisy was not a Catholic, and I was shocked at this lie.

TELLING LIES

★ Why has Tom told Myrtle that his wife is a Catholic?
★ How many different reasons can you think of for telling a lie?
★ Are lies always bad?

'When they get married,' continued Catherine, 'they'll go West for a while, until people stop talking about them anyway.'

'I almost married a man who was below[5] me, too,' said Mrs McKee suddenly.

'But at least you didn't marry him!' said Myrtle. 'I did!'

'She really should get away,' Catherine whispered in my ear.

---

1 object [əbˈdʒɛkt] (v.) 反對　　4 divorce [dəˈvɔrs] (n.) 離婚
2 dumb [dʌm] (a.)〔美〕笨的　5 below [bəˈlo] (prep.) 不配
3 cab [kæb] (n.)〔美〕計程車

We drank a second bottle of whiskey. Mr McKee went to sleep. I thought about going for a walk in the park, but each time I tried to leave I was pulled into another argument which stopped me.

Around midnight I heard Tom and Mrs Wilson discussing whether Mrs Wilson had the right to mention Daisy's name.

'Daisy! Daisy!' shouted Mrs Wilson. 'I'll say it when I want to.'

With a quick movement of his open hand, Tom Buchanan hit her on the face. Blood started pouring from her nose.

I picked up my hat and left. The next thing I remember was lying half-asleep in Pennsylvania Station, waiting for the four o'clock train.

CHAPTER THREE

There was music from Gatsby's house most nights. People came and went all the time. In the afternoons his guests swam in the sea or sunbathed on his beach while his two motorboats raced on the Sound. His Rolls Royce became a bus, carrying groups to and from the city, and his station wagon[1] met every train. On Mondays eight servants came to clean up the mess from the weekend.

Caterers[2] came regularly with colored lights to decorate the garden. They put up tables and filled them with cold meats, many different salads and pies. They set up a bar in the house. At seven o'clock the orchestra arrived. The swimmers had already left the beach and were changing into their evening clothes. More people arrived in their cars and soon the party was in full swing[3].

I believe that the first time I went to Gatsby's house, I was one of the few invited guests. People weren't invited – they arrived. But Gatsby had sent me a note in the morning. He would be honored[4] to see me at his party he wrote.

I felt rather uncomfortable at first because I didn't know anyone. I looked for Gatsby, but nobody knew where he was. I stood next to the bar and tried to hide my embarrassment by drinking. Then Jordan Baker came into the garden.

'Hello!' I shouted.

'I thought you might be here,' she replied. 'I remembered that you lived next door.'

---

1 station wagon 休旅車
2 caterer [ˈketərɚ] (n.) 承辦宴席的人；外燴業者
3 in full swing 漸入佳境；正順利進行中
4 honor [ˈɑnɚ] (v.) 使有榮幸

Two girls in yellow dresses walked past.

'Hello!' they cried. 'We're sorry you didn't win.'

Jordan had lost in the finals of a golf tournament the week before.

We walked round the garden and then we got some cocktails from the bar. We sat at a table with the two girls in yellow, and three men.

'Do you come to these parties often?' Jordan asked the girl next to her.

'Quite often,' she answered. 'Last time I tore[1] my dress on a chair. Gatsby asked for my name and address. In a week I got a package with an evening dress in it. Imagine! He paid $265 for a dress!'

'There's something strange about someone who does that,' said the other girl. 'He doesn't want any trouble with anybody.'

'Who doesn't?' I asked.

'Gatsby. Somebody told me that he killed a man once.'

'I don't know if that's true,' said the other girl. 'But he was a German spy during the war.'

'I heard that from a man who grew up with him in Germany,' said one of the men.

'Oh, no,' said the first girl, 'He was in the American army during the war.'

People started dancing to the music of the orchestra. Then a famous tenor sang in Italian and champagne was served in large glasses. Jordan and I went into the house to look for our host[2] but we didn't find him. We got another drink and sat down at a table with a man of about my age and a girl, who laughed at everything. I was enjoying myself now.

---

1 tear [tɛr] (v.) 扯破；撕開
2 host [host] (n.) 主人

When there was a pause in the entertainment, the man looked at me and smiled.

'Your face is familiar,' he said politely. 'Weren't you in the First Division[1] during the war?'

'Yes, I was.'

'I was too. I knew I'd seen you before.'

We talked about France. He told me that he had just bought a new boat. He was planning to go out in it in the morning.

'Want to come with me, old sport[2]?'

'What time?'

'I don't mind. You tell me.'

I turned to my new friend. 'This is an unusual party for me,' I said. 'I haven't seen the host. I live over there – ' and I pointed to my house 'and Gatsby sent me an invitation.'

He looked at me strangely.

'I'm Gatsby,' he said.

'What!' I exclaimed. 'Oh, I beg your pardon[3]!'

'I thought you knew, old sport. I'm afraid I'm not a very good host.'

At that moment a butler arrived and told Mr Gatsby that Chicago was calling on the phone.

'Excuse me, old sport,' he said. 'I'll see you later.'

I had expected Mr Gatsby to be fat, red-faced and middle-aged.

PARTIES

★ Do you like going to parties?
★ Do you give parties?

I turned to Jordan and asked, 'Who *is* he?'

'He's just a man named Gatsby.'

'No, I mean where is he from? What does he do?'

'Now *you've* started on that subject,' she answered, smiling. 'He told me once he was an Oxford man[4] . . . however, I don't believe it.'

Something in her voice reminded me of the other girl's 'I think he killed a man', and increased my curiosity[5]. Young men didn't arrive from nowhere and buy a palace on Long Island.

JAY GATSBY

★ Why is Gatsby's past such a mystery?
★ Where did he get his money from?

The orchestra started to play some jazz music. I looked around. Gatsby was standing on the steps of his house. He was looking at everyone with approving[6] eyes. He didn't look like a sinister[7] person with his attractive, tanned[8] face and short, tidy hair.

'Miss Baker?' It was Gatsby's butler. 'Excuse me, but Mr Gatsby would like to speak to you alone.'

'To me?' she exclaimed.

'Yes, madam.'

She got up, looking at me in surprise, and followed the butler.

---

1 division [də'vɪʒən] (n.) 〔軍〕師
2 old sport 老兄；弟兄（舊式用法）
3 I beg your pardon 請見諒
4 Oxford man 指上過牛津大學的人
5 curiosity [ˌkjʊrɪ'ɑsətɪ] (n.) 好奇心
6 approving [ə'pruvɪŋ] (a.) 贊成的
7 sinister ['sɪnɪstɚ] (a.) 邪惡的
8 tanned [tænd] (a.) 皮膚曬成棕褐色的

🎧 15   I was alone and it was almost two o'clock. A confused sound of voices was coming from a room that overlooked[1] the terrace. I went in. The room was full of people. One of the girls in yellow was playing the piano, and a tall red-haired lady from a famous chorus was singing.

People were leaving the party now. It was time for me to go too so I went into the hall to get my hat. Just then the door of the library opened and Jordan and Gatsby came out.

'I've just heard the most amazing thing,' she whispered to me, 'but I swore[2] I wouldn't tell.' She yawned[3]. 'Please come and see me.' And she hurried off to join her group, who were waiting for her at the door.

I went and joined the people around Gatsby. I wanted to explain to him that I had looked for him earlier in the evening. I also wanted to apologize for not recognizing him in the garden.

'Don't mention it, old sport,' he answered, putting his hand on my shoulder. His words and his gesture[4] were meant to be friendly and sincere but there was no real feeling behind them.

FRIENDS

★ Are Nick and Gatsby going to become good friends?
★ What is the most important quality of a good friend?
★ How do you try to be a good friend?

'And don't forget we're going out in my new boat tomorrow,' he added. 'I'll pick you up at nine o'clock.'

Then the butler said, 'Philadelphia wants you on the phone, sir.'

'Tell them I'll be right there. Good night old sport.'

'Good night,' I replied.

I walked home across the lawn. I stopped and turned round once. A small crescent[5] moon was shining over Gatsby's house. It was a beautiful clear night. I remembered the music and the laughter of the evening. The lights in the garden were still on but the house seemed very empty now.

---

1 overlook [ˌovəˈlʊk] (v.) 眺望;俯瞰
2 swear [swɛr] (v.) 發誓
3 yawn [jɔn] (v.) 打哈欠
4 gesture [ˈdʒɛstʃɚ] (n.) 姿勢;手勢
5 crescent [ˈkrɛsn̩t] (a.) 新月形的

I've given the impression that the events of these three nights were all that interested me that summer. That isn't true. Those three nights were weeks apart. Between them I led a very full and busy life. Most of the time I worked in New York. I made friends with the other young men in the office and had lunch with them in crowded restaurants. I even had a short love affair with a girl who worked in accounts[1], but when she went away on vacation I let the relationship end quietly. I usually had dinner at the Yale Club, and then I went upstairs to the library and read for an hour. After that, I often walked down Madison Avenue and across 33rd Street to the Pennsylvania Station. I began to like New York.

I didn't see Jordan Baker for a while, and then in the middle of the summer I met her again. At first I enjoyed going out with her. Because she was a golf champion everyone knew her name. Then I realized my feelings were changing. I wasn't in love with her but I felt tender[2] towards her. She was a strongly competitive woman. I remembered that she had once cheated[3] in a tournament that she was losing. However, I didn't let her know my feelings. I knew I had to end the relationship with the girl back home in the Midwest first. I have always been an honest person and I knew I couldn't continue to deceive[4] her.

1 account [əˋkaʊnt] (n.) 帳目
2 tender [ˋtɛndɚ] (a.) 溫情的
3 cheat [tʃit] (v.) 作弊
4 deceive [dɪˋsiv] (v.) 欺騙；蒙蔽

CHAPTER FOUR

At nine o'clock one morning in late July, Gatsby drove up to the front of my house and sounded the horn[5] of his car.

'Good morning, old sport,' he said when I opened the door. 'We're having lunch today and I thought we'd ride there together.'

I looked with admiration at his car.

'It's pretty, isn't it, old sport? Haven't you seen it before?'

'Yes, of course. It's gorgeous[6].'

Everybody knew Gatsby's car. It was a rich cream color, almost yellow and had green leather seats. There was plenty of space in it for all kinds of boxes – hat boxes, picnic boxes and tool boxes.

I got in and he drove off through West Egg.

I'd talked with him half a dozen[7] times in the last month and found, to my disappointment, that he had little to say. I no longer thought that he was an important person. He was just the owner of the big house next door. So I was surprised when he suddenly turned to me and said, 'What's your opinion of me, old sport?'

I didn't know what to say.

OPINIONS

★ How quickly do you form an opinion of a person?
★ Have you ever changed your first opinion of a person? Why?
★ Are your opinions influenced by other people's opinions?

---

5 horn [hɔrn] (n.) 喇叭
6 gorgeous [ˋgɔrdʒəs] (a.) 華麗的；〔口〕極好的
7 half a dozen 半打（即六個）

'I'm going to tell you about my life,' he continued. 'I don't want you to get the wrong idea from the stories you hear.'

So he knew about the strange things people said about him.

'I'll tell you the truth,' he said. 'I'm the son of some wealthy[1] people from the Midwest. I was brought up in America but educated at Oxford. All my ancestors[2] have been there. It's a family tradition. '

He said 'educated at Oxford' very quickly and checked my reaction with a sideways[3] look. Now I understood why Jordan didn't believe this story. Perhaps there really was something sinister about him.

'But then all my family died and I inherited[4] lots of money.'

I looked at him. For a moment I thought he was joking but his face was very serious.

'After that,' he continued, 'I lived in all the big European cities – Paris, Venice, Rome. I collected rubies[5], went hunting, painted a little and tried to forget something very sad that happened to me long ago.'

I didn't know whether to believe him or not but I let him go on with his story.

'Then the war started, old sport. I tried very hard to die, but I seemed to have an enchanted[6] life.'

He'd won many medals. He took one out of his pocket and showed it to me.

'Turn it over,' he said.

On the back of the medal I read: 'Major Jay Gatsby. For Valor[7] Extraordinary[8].'

He also showed me a photograph of himself at Oxford.

'The man on my left is the Earl[9] of Dorcaster,' he said.

So it was all true.

'I'm going to ask you to do me a big favor today,' he said. 'I didn't want you to think I was just a nobody. I'm usually among strangers because I'm always moving from place to place trying to forget the sad thing that happened to me.'

---

1 wealthy [ˈwɛlθɪ] (a.) 富有的
2 ancestor [ˈænsɛstɚ] (n.) 祖先
3 sideways [ˈsaɪdˌwez] (a.) 向一邊的
4 inherit [ɪnˈhɛrɪt] (v.) 繼承
5 ruby [ˈrubɪ] (n.) 紅寶石
5 enchanted [ɪnˈtʃæntɪd] (a.) 吸引人的
7 valor [ˈvælɚ] (n.) 英勇
8 extraordinary [ɪkˈstrɔrdn̩ˌɛrɪ] (a.) 非凡的
9 earl [ɝl] (n.) (英國的)伯爵

He hesitated.

'You'll hear about it this afternoon. I know you're having tea with Miss Baker, and she's agreed to tell you everything.'

This annoyed me a little. I hadn't invited Jordan to tea to talk about Jay Gatsby.

Gatsby raced through Long Island City. Then just before we reached the bridge, I heard the jug-jug-SPAT! noise of a motorcycle next to us. It was a policeman. He wanted us to stop. Gatsby slowed down, took a white card out of his pocket and showed it to him.

'Alright, old sport?'

'Sorry, Mr Gatsby, sir! I'll recognize you next time.'

'What was that?' I asked. 'The Oxford photograph?'

'I did the chief of police a favor once. Now he sends me a Christmas card every year,' he replied.

We went to a restaurant on Forty-second Street, where Gatsby introduced me to his friend Wolfsheim.

'This place is nice,' Wolfsheim said, 'but I like the Metropole across the street better. It's full of memories. Faces and friends dead and gone forever. I can't forget the night they shot Rosy Rosenthal there. There were six of us at the table, and Rosy had eaten and drunk a lot all evening. Then the waiter came up to him and said that somebody wanted to speak to him outside. He stood up and said to me 'Don't let that waiter take away my coffee!' Then he went outside. They shot him three times and drove away.'

'I remember,' I said.

Wolfsheim turned to me.

'I understand you're looking for a business connection,' he said.

Gatsby answered for me, 'No, this isn't the man. He's just a friend. We'll talk about that another time.'

'I'm sorry. I made a mistake.' He seemed disappointed.

Our food arrived and Mr Wolfsheim started to eat hungrily.

Gatsby leaned towards me. 'I'm sorry, old sport. I think I made you angry this morning.'

'I don't like mysteries,' I replied coldly. 'Why did you involve Miss Baker? Can't you tell me yourself?'

'Oh, she doesn't mind,' he said.

Then he looked at his watch, jumped up suddenly and hurried from the room.

WOLFSHEIM

★ Who do you think Wolfsheim's friends were?
★ What do you know about America in the 1920s?

'He has to telephone,' Wolfsheim explained. He followed Gatsby with his eyes. 'A handsome man and a perfect gentleman, isn't he?'

'Yes.'

'He's an Oxford man.'

'Oh.'

'He went to Oxford College in England. Do you know it?'

'I've heard of it.'

'It's one of the most famous colleges in the world.'

'Have you known Gatsby long?' I inquired.

'For several years,' he answered. 'I met him just after the war. After talking to him for an hour, I knew he was a gentleman – the kind of man you would introduce to your mother, or your sister.'

'Yes.'

'Yeah, Gatsby's careful about women. He would never look at a friend's wife.'

THINK!

★ What impression of Gatsby is Meyer Wolfsheim trying to give Nick?
★ What do you think the relationship between Gatsby and Wolfsheim is?

When Gatsby returned, Wolfsheim drank his coffee and got up. 'I enjoyed my lunch,' he said, 'but now I'm going to leave you two young men together.'

'Don't hurry, Meyer!' Gatsby said, but there was no enthusiasm in his voice.

'You're very polite, but I'm an old man,' Wolfsheim replied. 'You stay here and discuss your sports and your ladies.'

After he'd left, Gatsby said, 'Everyone in New York knows him.'

'Is he an actor?'

'No, Meyer Wolfsheim's a gambler[1].' Gatsby hesitated, then added coolly, 'He's the man who fixed[2] the World Series[3] in 1919.'

I was shocked. I had never imagined that only one man was responsible for cheating fifty million people.

'How did he do that?' I asked.

'He just saw an opportunity.'

'Why isn't he in jail[4]?'

'They can't get him, old sport. He's a smart[5] man.'

STEALING

★ Is it worse to steal from one person or from fifty million people?

I paid. As the waiter brought my change I saw Tom Buchanan.

'Come with me,' I said. 'I've got to say hello to someone.'

Tom jumped up when he saw me.

'Where've you been?' he demanded[6]. 'Daisy's furious[7] because you haven't phoned.'

'This is Mr Gatsby, Mr Buchanan.'

They shook hands briefly, and I saw a strange look of embarrassment on Gatsby's face.

'Why did you come this far to eat?' asked Tom.

---

1 gambler [ˈgæmblɚ] (n.) 賭徒
2 fix [fɪks] (v.) 〔口〕操縱賄賂
3 World Series 美國職棒大聯盟
   的年度總冠軍賽
4 jail [dʒel] (n.) 監獄
5 smart [smɑrt] (a.) 聰明的
6 demand [dɪˈmænd] (v.) 查問
7 furious [ˈfjʊərɪəs] (a.) 狂怒的

'I've been having lunch with Mr Gatsby.'

I turned towards Gatsby, but he was no longer there.

'One October day in 1917' (said Jordan Baker that afternoon in the tea garden at the Plaza Hotel) – I was walking past Daisy's house. She was eighteen and the most popular girl in Louisville. She was sitting in her little white car with an officer in uniform.

'Hello, Jordan,' she called.

The officer was looking at her in a very special way. His name was Jay Gatsby. I met him again four years later on Long Island but I didn't realize it was the same man.

I didn't see Daisy very often because I began to play in tournaments, but I heard about her. Her mother had stopped her from going to New York to say goodbye to a soldier who was going overseas[1]. The next year she married Tom.'

RELATIONSHIPS

* What is the 'sad thing' that happened to Jay Gatsby long ago?
* What do you think the relationship between Jay Gatsby and Daisy is?
* Why do you think Daisy's mother stopped her from going to New York to say goodbye to Gatsby?
* Do you think parents should influence their children's relationships?

1 overseas ['ovɚ'siz] (adv.) 在國外

CHAPTER FIVE

I arrived home at two o'clock in the morning. As my taxi left, I saw Gatsby walking towards me.

'Let's go to Coney Island, old sport, in my car.'

'It's too late,' I replied.

'Well, what about a swim in my pool! I haven't used it this summer yet.'

'I must go to bed.'

'All right.'

He waited, looking at me.

'I talked with Miss Baker,' I said. 'I'm going to phone Daisy tomorrow and invite her to tea. Which day suits[1] you?'

'Which day suits YOU?' he replied quickly. 'I don't want to cause you any trouble.'

'How about the day after tomorrow?'

He paused before answering. 'I must cut the grass first.' He looked at the grass in my garden. He hesitated again. 'Oh, there's another little thing . . .'

'We can do it next week if you want,' I said. I thought he needed more time.

'No, it isn't that.' He didn't know how to continue. Then he said, 'You don't make much money, do you, old sport?'

'Not very much.'

'Well, I run a little business and I think I have something that might interest you. You might earn some money. Something just between you and me, you understand.'

The offer was clearly in return for my help so I refused.

THE OFFER

★ Explain what Nick means.
★ What does Gatsby's offer tell us about Gatsby?

I rang Daisy the next morning and invited her to come to tea.

'Don't bring Tom,' I warned her.

It was raining on the day we had fixed to have tea. A man arrived at eleven o'clock to cut the grass in my garden (Gatsby's lawn was always perfect). A little later an enormous quantity of flowers was delivered.

At three o'clock the front door opened and Gatsby hurried in. He looked anxious.

'Have you got everything you need for tea?' he asked.

I took him into the kitchen and showed him the lemon cakes I had bought that morning.

'Are they all right?'

'Of course! They're fine, – old sport,' he said, but I could see he was disappointed.

---

1 suit [sut] (v.) 適合

We went into the living room where he sat down. From time to time he looked through the windows at the rain. Finally he got up and said he was going home.

'Nobody's coming to tea. It's too late! I can't wait all day.'

'Don't be silly. It's only two minutes to four.'

He sat down miserably[1] and, at the same time, a car drove up to my house.

I went out into the garden. Daisy looked at me and smiled happily. I helped her out of the car.

'Are you in love with me?' she said softly in my ear. 'If not, why did I have to come alone?'

'That's a secret.'

We went in. To my surprise the living room was empty. Then there was a knock at the door. I opened it. Gatsby was standing there in the rain. He disappeared quickly into the living room. I waited at the door. After a moment of silence, Daisy laughed and said in a clear, artificial[2] voice, 'I'm very glad to see you again.'

I closed the door and joined them in the living room. Gatsby was standing and staring[3] at Daisy. She was sitting, frightened but composed[4], on the edge of a chair.

'We've met before,' Gatsby said.

'Not for many years,' Daisy added quickly.

'Five years next November,' said Gatsby automatically.

🎧 I sat and talked to Daisy as we drank our tea and ate the lemon cakes. Gatsby was quiet but his anxious, unhappy eyes moved continuously from me to Daisy. I left them together after a while.

When I went back in, they were sitting on the couch, looking at each other. All their embarrassment had gone. Daisy's face was covered with tears. But there was a change in Gatsby that really surprised me. He radiated[5] a feeling of joy that filled the room.

CHANGES OF FEELINGS

★ Think of situations when your feelings might change
  • from anxiety to joy.
  • from joy to unhappiness.

'Hello, old sport,' he said.

'It's stopped raining.'

'Has it?' he said. Then to Daisy: 'It's stopped raining.'

'I'm glad, Jay,' she answered, her voice showing her unexpected joy.

Then suddenly, 'I want you and Daisy to come to my house. I'd like to show her around.'

Outside in the garden, Daisy pointed and said, 'Is that it? That huge place *there*?'

'Do you like it?'

'I love it. Do you really live there alone?'

'I invite lots of interesting and famous people, so it's full night and day.'

1 miserably ['mɪzərəblɪ] (adv.) 令人難受地
2 artificial [ˌɑrtə'fɪʃəl] (a.) 造作的；不自然的
3 stare [stɛr] (v.) 盯；凝視
4 composed [kəm'pozd] (a.) 平靜的
5 radiate ['redɪˌet] (v.) 流露出

He showed her all the beautiful sitting rooms, the music rooms and the library. Daisy admired everything and Gatsby seemed to revalue[1] everything according to the response it got from her eyes. He hadn't stopped looking at her once.

In his bedroom, we stood at the window and looked at the Sound. It had started to rain again.

'It's a pity it's so misty[2]', he said. 'On a clear day I can see your house across the bay. At night there's a green light at the end of your dock.'

---

1 revalue [rɪˋvæljʊ] (v.) 重新評價
2 misty [ˋmɪstɪ] (a.) 有霧的

Daisy put her arm through his as they looked out. The green light had been his connection with Daisy. Now that she was here it had lost its significance.

In the west there were pink and golden clouds above the sea.

'Look,' she whispered. 'I'd like to get one of those pink clouds and put you in it and push you around.'

I tried to go then but they wanted me to stay.

'I know what we'll do,' said Gatsby. 'We'll ask Klipspringer to play the piano.'

I had often seen Klipspringer in the pool and on the beach. Now, as we sat in the music room, he played love songs to us.

I looked at Gatsby and Daisy and I saw that they had forgotten me. He was holding her hand and she was saying something in his ear. He turned towards her, his face full of emotion. I got up and left them there together.

CHAPTER SIX

Jay Gatsby was really James Gatz, the son of unsuccessful farmers in North Dakota. He changed his name when he was seventeen, the same moment he saw Dan Cody's yacht on Lake Superior. Cody was a fifty-year-old multi-millionaire who had made his money in silver and copper[1]. To Gatz, the yacht represented all the beauty and glamour in the world. He already had a clear idea of the kind of person he wanted to be – and he had probably already invented his new name. He was just waiting for the right moment to start out on his new career. And this was it. He obviously managed to impress Cody because when the yacht left for the West Indies, Gatsby was on it.

Cody soon discovered that the young boy was quick to learn and extremely ambitious. He did all the jobs there are to do on a yacht, and he was also Cody's secretary. Five years later when Cody died, Jay Gatsby was no longer just an idea in a young boy's imagination. He was a real person.

I didn't see or hear from him for several weeks. I was spending a lot of time in New York with Jordan. But one Sunday afternoon, I went to his house. About two minutes later we heard the sound of horses' hooves[2] and Tom Buchanan arrived. I was a little surprised to see him.

He had ridden there with two friends – a man named Sloane and a pretty woman, who seemed to know Gatsby.

'I'm pleased to see you,' said Gatsby, standing on his porch. 'I'm delighted that you decided to pay me a visit.'

---

1 copper [ˈkɑpɚ] (n.) 銅
2 hoof [huf] (n.) 蹄

I'm sure that they didn't really care if he was pleased or not. They only wanted to rest after their ride. Gatsby knew that too, but Tom's presence made him nervous.

He called the butler and ordered drinks. Then he said, 'I believe we've met somewhere before, Mr Buchanan.'

'Oh, yes,' Tom replied politely. He obviously didn't remember the occasion. 'Yes. I remember it well.'

'About two weeks ago.'

'That's right. You were with Nick.'

'I know your wife.'

'Do you?' Tom turned to me. 'Do you live near here, Nick?'

'Next door.'

'We must go now,' said Mr Sloane. 'Come on,' he said to the woman.

I walked to the porch with Tom.

'I wonder where he met Daisy,' he said. 'Women go out too much these days. They meet all kinds of strange men.'

MEETING NEW PEOPLE

★ How do you meet new people?
★ What do you talk about when you meet a new person?

Tom was obviously worried about this because the following Saturday night he came with Daisy to Gatsby's party. We all walked together among the hundreds of people.

'Look around,' said Gatsby. 'You must see many people you've heard about.'

Tom's arrogant eyes looked around.

'We don't go out much,' he said. 'In fact, I was just thinking I don't know anyone here.'

Gatsby took them from group to group.

'I've never met so many celebrities,' Daisy exclaimed.

Daisy and Gatsby danced. Then they walked slowly over to my house and sat on the steps for half an hour. Daisy asked me to stay in the garden.

'In case there's a fire, or something like that,' she said.

Tom appeared from nowhere as we were sitting down to supper together.

'Do you mind if I eat with some people over there?' he said. 'A man's saying some interesting things.'

'Go ahead,' answered Daisy. 'And if you want to make a note of some addresses, here's my little gold pencil . . .'

She turned round a few minutes later. Tom was sitting with a girl.

'Common[1] but pretty,' Daisy told me.

I knew that, except for the half hour she'd been alone with Gatsby, she wasn't having a good time.

I sat on the front steps with them while they waited for their car.

'Who is this Gatsby?' demanded Tom suddenly. 'Some big bootlegger[2]?'

'Where did you hear that?' I inquired.

'I didn't hear it. I guessed it. A lot of these newly[3] rich people are just big bootleggers.'

He was silent for a moment.

'It must be hard work to get such a strange collection of people together at a party!'

'They're more interesting than the people we know,' said Daisy.

'You didn't look very interested.'

'Well, I was,' she replied.

'I'd like to know who he is and what he does,' insisted Tom. 'And I think I'll find out.'

'I can tell you right now,' she answered. 'He owned a lot of drugstores[4].'

Their car came up the drive[5].

'Good night, Nick,' said Daisy.

---

1 common [ˋkɑmən] (a.) 普通的；平凡的
2 bootlegger [ˋbut͵lɛgɚ] (n.) 私販酒類的人
3 newly [ˋnjulɪ] (adv.) 最近；近來
4 drugstore [ˋdrʌg͵stor] (n.)〔美〕藥房雜貨物店
5 drive [draɪv] (n.) 從大門口到屋宅的車道

I stayed late because Gatsby had asked me to wait for him. When he came into the garden, his eyes were bright but he looked tired.

'Daisy didn't like it,' he said immediately.

'Of course she did.'

He was silent, and I guessed he was depressed.

'I feel far away from her,' he said. 'It's hard to make her understand.'

'What do you mean?'

He wanted Daisy to go to Tom and say 'I never loved you.' The last four years could be removed with those words. Then, when she was free, they would go back to Louisville and get married – just as he had planned five years ago.

'She doesn't understand,' he said. 'She understood before but now she doesn't . . .'

He stopped and began to walk up and down.

'You shouldn't ask too much of her,' I suggested. 'You can't repeat the past.'

'Of course you can!' he cried. 'I'm going to fix everything just the way it was before.'

He talked a lot about the past that night. He told me about the time he had first kissed Daisy one autumn night five years before. He imagined then that he could have everything he wanted. He could see then what his life could be like. But his life had been confused and without order since then. He had lost something – an idea of himself perhaps. If he could go back and do everything again slowly, perhaps he would discover what that something was.

CHAPTER SEVEN

One Saturday night the lights in Gatsby's house didn't go on. Cars arrived, stayed for just a minute then drove away again. I wondered if he was ill so I went to find out. A butler I didn't recognize answered the door.

'Is Mr Gatsby sick?'

'No,' he said rudely.

'I was worried. Tell him Mr Carraway came.'

'Carraway. All right, I'll tell him.'

Later my housekeeper told me that my neighbor had sent all his old servants away and replaced them with just six others. She didn't think they were real servants.

The next day Gatsby phoned me.

'Are you going away?' I asked. 'I hear you fired[1] the servants.'

'I wanted people who don't gossip[2]. Daisy often comes over in the afternoons.'

So he had changed the servants because she disapproved[3] of them.

'She wants to know if you'll come to lunch at her house tomorrow. Miss Baker will be there.'

Soon after, Daisy phoned. She was happy that I had agreed to go. I felt that something was wrong between her and Gatsby.

GATSBY AND DAISY

★ What could be wrong between Gatsby and Daisy?

The next day was very warm. When Gatsby and I got to the Buchanan's house, a maid showed us into a darkened sitting room. Daisy and Jordan were lying on an enormous couch while fans cooled the air around them. Tom wasn't there.

'We can't move,' they said.

Gatsby stood in the middle of the red carpet and looked around, fascinated.

Then Tom came in. He put out his hand.

'Mr Gatsby! I'm glad to see you . . . Nick . . .'

'Make us a cold drink,' cried Daisy.

As soon as he was out of the room she got up, went over to Gatsby and kissed him on the mouth.

'You know I love you,' she whispered.

---

1 fire [faɪr] (v.) 解雇
2 gossip [ˈgɑsəp] (v.) 講閒話
3 disapprove [ˌdɪsəˈpruv] (v.) 不贊成;不同意

Tom came back with the drinks.

'They certainly look cool,' said Gatsby as Tom gave him one.

We drank and talked about the weather. Then Tom said to Gatsby, 'Come outside and have a look around.'

They went out on the verandah[1] and I followed.

We looked out over the Sound. Gatsby pointed across the bay. 'My house is over there. Exactly opposite yours.'

'That's right,' Tom replied.

We stayed there for a few more minutes then we went back inside to a darkened dining room and had lunch.

Afterwards Daisy said, 'What shall we do this afternoon? It's so hot and everything's so confused. Let's go to town[2]!'

Gatsby's eyes turned towards her.

'Ah,' she cried, 'you look so cool.'

They looked at each other, as if nobody else was there.

She was telling him she loved him with her eyes. Tom saw it. He was very surprised. He looked at Gatsby, and then at Daisy.

---

1 verandah [vəˈrændə] (n.) 陽台
2 town [taʊn] (n.) 在此指紐約市

'Come on,' he said quickly, 'we're going to town.'

He got up, but nobody else moved.

'What? Now?' Daisy asked. 'Dressed like this?'

Tom didn't say anything.

'Oh, alright. But we'll need time to get ready.'

She and Jordan went upstairs while we three men stood outside.

'Shall we take something to drink?' shouted Daisy from an upstairs window.

'I'll get a bottle of whiskey,' answered Tom and went inside.

🎧 He came out a few minutes later followed by Daisy and Jordan.

'Let's go in my car,' suggested Gatsby.

'No, you take my coupé[1] and let me drive your car.'

Gatsby didn't like the idea.

'Come on, Daisy,' said Tom, leading her towards Gatsby's car. 'I'll take you in this.'

He opened the door, but she moved away.

'You take Nick and Jordan. We'll follow in the coupé,' she said, moving towards Gatsby.

So Jordan, Tom and I got into Gatsby's car and Tom drove off.

'Did you see that?' he asked.

'See what?'

'You think I'm pretty dumb, don't you?' he said. 'Perhaps I am, but I've investigated[2] Gatsby's past.'

'And you found out he was an Oxford man,' said Jordan.

'An Oxford man!' he repeated with contempt[3].

'If you don't believe it, why did you invite him?' demanded Jordan.

'Daisy invited him. She knew him before we were married.'

'Do we have enough gasoline[4]?' I asked.

'Enough to get us to town,' said Tom.

'There's a garage over there,' said Jordan. 'I don't want to get stuck[5] in this heat[6].'

TOM

★ How does Tom feel?

★ Why did he want to drive Gatsby's car?

★ Does Tom suspect that Daisy had a relationship with Gatsby before she married?

Tom stopped impatiently under Wilson's sign. A moment later the owner appeared.

'Give me some gas!' shouted Tom.

'I'm sick,' said Wilson without moving.

'What's the matter?'

'I'm run down[7],' answered Wilson. 'I need money badly. What about your old car?'

'Do you like this one?' asked Tom. 'I bought it last week.'

'It's a nice color but it's too expensive for me.'

'What do you want money for anyway?'

'I've been here too long. My wife and I want to go West.'

'Your wife wants to go West?' exclaimed Tom. The news surprised him.

'She's talked about it for years. Now she's going whether[8] she wants to or not.'

The coupé flashed[9] past us. Gatsby and Daisy waved.

'I've just understood something strange,' said Wilson. 'That's why I want to leave and why I'm interested in the car.'

'What do I owe[10] you?'

'A dollar twenty[11].'

I realized that Wilson didn't suspect[12] Tom. He'd discovered that Myrtle had another life and this had made him sick. I stared at Tom. Tom had made a similar discovery less than an hour earlier.

'I'll send that car to you tomorrow,' said Tom.

---

1 coupe [ˋkupe] (n.) 雙門小轎車
2 investigate [ɪnˋvɛstəˏget] (v.) 調查
3 contempt [kənˋtɛmpt] (n.) 輕視；蔑視
4 gasoline [ˋgæsəˏlin] (n.) 〔美〕汽油
5 stick [stɪk] (v.) 被困住
6 heat [hit] (n.) 高溫；炎熱
7 run down 身體虛弱
8 whether [ˋhwɛðɚ] (conj.) 是否
9 flash [flæʃ] (v.) 閃光
10 owe [o] (v.) 欠錢
11 twenty 在此指 20 分錢
12 suspect [səˋspɛkt] (v.) 懷疑

From a window over the garage Myrtle Wilson was looking down. Her eyes were fixed on Jordan, however, not Tom, and they were full of jealousy. She thought that Jordan was his wife.

It was obvious that Tom was in a panic. An hour ago, his wife and his mistress[1] were both secure. Now he was losing control of both of them. He put his foot down hard on the accelerator[2]. Soon we could see the blue coupé. Daisy waved her arms at us. She was telling us to stop.

'Where are we going?' she cried.

'Let's go to the movies,' Jordan suggested.

'It's too hot,' Daisy replied. 'You go if you like. We'll drive around and meet you later.'

'I'm not going to argue here in the street,' Tom said angrily. 'Follow me to the Plaza Hotel.'

There we hired[3] a large, hot, sitting room. There was no air in the room.

'Open another window,' ordered Daisy.

'Forget about the heat,' said Tom impatiently. 'You make it worse by complaining.'

He took out the whiskey and put it on the table.

'Leave her alone, old sport,' remarked Gatsby. 'You wanted to come to town.'

'That's a great expression of yours, isn't it?' said Tom sharply.

'What is?'

'This "old sport". Where did you get that from?'

'Tom!' said Daisy, 'If you're going to make personal remarks I won't stay. Order some ice and we can have mint[4] juleps[5].'

---

1 mistress [ˈmɪstrɪs] (n.) 情婦
2 accelerator [ækˈsɛləˌretɚ] (n.) 油門
3 hire [haɪr] (v.) 租
4 mint [mɪnt] (n.) 薄荷
5 julep [ˈdʒulɪp] (n.) 〔美〕冰鎮薄荷酒

Tom ordered the ice and we made small talk[1] for a while. Then Tom said, 'Mr Gatsby, I understand you're an Oxford man.'

'Well, I went there.'

'I'd like to know when.'

'It was in 1919. But I only stayed for five months, so I'm not really an Oxford man.'

The waiter arrived with the mint and the ice.

'After the War,' Gatsby continued, 'they gave some officers the opportunity to go to a university in England or France. The officers could choose which one.'

Not for the first time, I changed my opinion of him.

'Open the whiskey, Tom,' Daisy ordered, 'and I'll make you a mint julep. Then you won't feel so stupid.'

ANGER

★ Do you get angry quickly?
★ What kind of things make you angry?
★ What do you do when you are angry?

'Wait a minute,' Tom said sharply[2]. 'I want to ask Mr Gatsby another question.'

'Go on,' Gatsby said politely.

'What kind of row[3] are you trying to cause in my house?'

They were being open at last, and Gatsby was happy.

'He isn't causing a row.' said Daisy. 'You are. Please! Try and control yourself!'

'What! Control myself!,' Tom shouted. 'Must I sit here and let Mr Nobody from Nowhere take my wife away?'

'I've got something to tell you, old sport,' began Gatsby.

'Please don't!' Daisy interrupted. She guessed what his intentions[4] were. 'Please! Let's go home. Why don't we all go home?'

'That's a good idea,' I said and got up. 'Come on, Tom. Nobody wants a drink.'

'I want to know what Mr Gatsby has to tell me,' Tom said.

'Your wife doesn't love you,' said Gatsby. 'She has never loved you. She loves me.'

'You're crazy!' exclaimed Tom.

Gatsby stood up. His face was alive with excitement now.

'She only married you because I was poor and she was tired of waiting for me,' he cried. 'It was a terrible mistake. In her heart she has never loved anyone except me!'

Jordan and I tried to leave, but Tom and Gatsby asked us to stay.

'What are you talking about?' asked Tom. 'I want to know.'

'I've told you,' said Gatsby. 'We've been in love for five years.'

Tom turned to Daisy. 'How often have you met him?'

'We couldn't meet,' said Gatsby. 'But both of us loved each other all that time, old sport. And you didn't know! It sometimes made me laugh.'

'Is that all?' asked Tom. Then he exploded, 'You're crazy! I can't speak about what happened five years ago because I didn't know Daisy then. But all the rest is a lie. Daisy loved me when she married me and she loves me now.'

'No,' said Gatsby, shaking his head.

'She does. Sometimes she has foolish[5] ideas and she doesn't know what she's doing,' he said. 'But I love Daisy. Sometimes I go off and have an "adventure[6]" and make a fool of myself. But I always come back. And in my heart I love her all the time.'

---

1 small talk 閒聊
2 sharply [ˈʃɑrplɪ] (adv.) 尖銳地
3 row [raʊ] (n.)〔口〕口角；爭吵
4 intention [ɪnˈtɛnʃən] (n.) 意圖；意向
5 foolish [ˈfulɪʃ] (a.) 愚蠢的
6 adventure [ədˈvɛntʃɚ] (n.) 奇遇

'You're revolting[1], said Daisy. She turned to me, 'Do you know why we left Chicago? I'm surprised that you didn't hear the story of his little "adventure" there.'

'Daisy, that doesn't matter,' said Gatsby. 'Just tell the truth – you never loved him.'

She looked at Jordan and me for help, as though she realized at last what she was doing. But it was too late.

DAISY

★ Does Daisy know which man she loves?
★ Why might she love Gatsby? Why might she love Tom?
★ Which man will she choose?

'I have never loved him,' she said with a reluctance[2] that we all noticed.

'Not at Kapiolani[3]?' demanded Tom.

'No.'

'Not that day I carried you down from the Punch Bowl[4] to keep your shoes dry?' There was a tenderness in Tom's voice.

'Please don't,' she said. Then turning to Gatsby, she started to cry. 'You want too much. I love you now – isn't that enough? I can't help what's past. I did love him once – but I loved you, too.'

'You loved me, TOO?' Gatsby repeated.

'Even that's not true,' said Tom. 'There are things between me and Daisy that you'll never know – that we'll never forget.'

Gatsby looked shocked. 'I want to speak to Daisy alone,' he said. 'She's upset[5] now.'

45 'Even alone I can't say I have never loved Tom,' Daisy admitted. 'It would be a lie.'

'Of course it would,' agreed Tom. 'I'm going to take better care of you from now on.'

'You don't understand,' said Gatsby. 'Daisy's leaving you.' 'Nonsense[6].'

'I am, though,' Daisy forced herself to say.

'She's not leaving me!' Tom said firmly. 'Certainly not for a thief.'

'This is all too much for me!' cried Daisy. 'Let's go.'

---

1 revolting [rɪˈvoltɪŋ] (a.) 令人噁心的
2 reluctance [rɪˈlʌktəns] (n.) 不情願
3 Kapiolani 檀香山的一處大公園
4 Punch Bowl 位於檀香山的一座死火山
5 upset [ʌpˈsɛt] (a.) 心煩的
6 nonsense [ˈnɑnsɛns] (int.) 胡說

Tom leaned close towards Gatsby. 'I know you're a friend of Meyer Wolfsheim. I've done some investigating – and I'm going to continue tomorrow.'

'Do what you like, old sport.'

'I know what your drugstores are.' Tom turned to Jordan and me. 'I found out that they bought a lot of drugstores together here and in Chicago. They sell alcohol in them. That's one of his businesses. But he's starting something bigger now. I knew he was a bootlegger when I saw him. And I was right!'

I looked at Daisy and saw the terror in her face as her eyes moved from Gatsby to her husband. Then I looked at Jordan. Her face had the bored expression I knew well. Then at Gatsby. His cool, self-confident[1] manner[2] had gone.

SELF-CONFIDENCE

★ How do people behave when they are self-confident?
★ And when they lose their self-confidence?
★ What kind of experiences help to build a person's self-confidence?

He began talking excitedly to Daisy. He denied[3] everything, defended his name. But it was no use. She wasn't listening to him. '*Please*, Tom! I can't take any more[4].'

1 self-confident [sɛlfˋkɑnfədənt] (a.) 自信的
2 manner [ˋmænɚ] (n.) 態度;方式
3 deny [dɪˋnaɪ] (v.) 否認
4 can't take any more 忍無可忍
5 flirtation [flɝˋteʃən] (n.) 調情;打情罵俏

Her frightened eyes showed that her intentions and courage had definitely gone.

'Go home, Daisy,' said Tom. 'Gatsby will take you in his car. He won't annoy you. He knows that his silly flirtation[5] is over.'

And they left without a word. It was seven o'clock when we got into the coupé with Tom and drove to Long Island. He talked and laughed continuously, but he seemed to be very far away from Jordan and me. As we passed over the bridge her pale face fell against my shoulder and she took my hand. That day was my birthday. I was thirty.

CHAPTER EIGHT

At five o'clock, Michaelis, a young Greek man who ran the café next to Wilson's garage, went round for a chat. He found Wilson in the office. He looked very ill. He tried to persuade him to go to bed, but Wilson said he didn't want to miss any customers. Suddenly there was a terrible noise from upstairs.

'My wife's locked in,' explained Wilson calmly. 'She's going to stay there till we move away.'

Michaelis was surprised to hear words like those from his neighbor. He tried to find out what had happened but Wilson didn't want to explain. Just then some workmen went into his café, so he left to serve them. He came outside again just after seven and heard Mrs Wilson's voice, loud and angry, downstairs in the garage. She was shouting at her husband.

A moment later she ran out into the dark night. Before he could do anything it was over.

The 'death car', as the newspapers called it, didn't stop. It came out of the darkness, moved sideways for a moment, then disappeared around the next bend. Michaelis wasn't even sure of its color. He told the policeman later that it was light green. Another car heading for New York stopped and its driver hurried back to where Myrtle Wilson lay dead in the road.

We saw some cars and the crowd before we arrived at the scene.

'Crash!' said Tom. 'Good. Wilson'll have some business.'

He stopped at the garage.

'We'll take a look,' he said.

A wailing[1] sound was coming from the garage – it was Wilson. 'Oh, my God!' he cried over and over again.

'There's some bad trouble here,' said Tom, trying to look over the heads of the crowd.

Suddenly he made a strange sound and started pushing through the people. Jordan and I followed. Myrtle's body lay in a blanket[2] on a table by the wall. Tom was bending over her. Tom turned to the policeman, who was writing names in a little book.

'What happened?'

'A car hit her. She was killed instantly.'

'Killed instantly,' repeated Tom.

ROAD ACCIDENTS

★ What are some of the reasons for road accidents?
★ What can be done to reduce the number of accidents?

'She ran into the road,' said Michaelis. 'There were two cars. The one coming from New York hit her.'

Another man said, 'It was a big, new, yellow car.'

'Did you see the accident?'

'No, but the car passed me down the road. It was going very fast.'

Some of this conversation reached Wilson.

'You don't have to tell me! I know what kind of car it was!' he shouted.

The muscles in Tom's shoulders tensed. He walked over to Wilson and took hold of him.

'Pull yourself together[3],' he said quietly. 'I got here a minute ago, from New York. I was bringing you that coupé. That yellow car I was driving this afternoon wasn't mine.'

The policeman looked over at Tom.

'What's that?' he demanded.

'I'm a friend,' answered Tom. 'He says he recognized the car that did it. It was a yellow car.'

'What color's your car?' asked the policeman suspiciously.

'It's a blue coupé.'

'We've come straight from New York,' I said.

Someone who'd been behind us confirmed this and the policeman turned away.

Tom helped Wilson back into the office, where he sat down in a chair. Then he came back.

'Will somebody sit with him?' he asked.

Two men went in and Tom closed the door.

'Let's get out of here,' he whispered to me.

Tom drove slowly at first, then he put his foot down on the accelerator and the coupé raced through the night. I heard a sobbing[4] noise and saw that there were tears running down his face.

'The coward[5]!' he said. His voice was shaking with emotion. 'He didn't even stop.'

When we got to his house, Tom looked up at the second floor. The lights were on.

'Daisy's here,' he said. Then, 'I forgot to drop you in West Egg, Nick.'

1 wail [wel] (v.) 嚎啕；嗚咽
2 blanket [ˋblæŋkɪt] (n.) 毛毯；毯子
3 pull yourself together 控制自己的情緒；冷靜下來
4 sob [sɑb] (v.) 嗚咽；啜泣
5 coward [ˋkauəd] (n.) 懦夫；膽怯者

He was calm and serious now. The emotion had gone.

'There's nothing we can do tonight. I'll telephone for a taxi to take you home.'

He opened the door.

'Come in. You can wait in the kitchen. Have something to eat – if you want.'

'No, thanks. I'll wait outside.'

Jordan put her hand on my arm.

'Don't you want to come in, Nick?'

'No, thanks.'

I was feeling a little sick and wanted to be alone. Jordan didn't go in immediately.

'It's only half-past nine,' she said.

But I'd had enough of them for today, even Jordan. She looked at my face and understood. She turned and ran into the house.

JORDAN BAKER

★ What do we know about Jordan Baker?
★ Do you think Nick will continue to see Jordan?
★ How important is the character of Jordan in the story?

I sat on the steps with my head in my hands while the butler phoned for a taxi.

Then I walked down the drive away from the house to wait by the gate.

Suddenly Gatsby stepped from between two bushes on to the path.

'What are you doing?' I asked.

'Just standing here, old sport,' he said. 'Did you see any trouble on the road?'

'Yes.'

'Was she killed?'

'Yes.'

'I thought so. I told Daisy. She took it quite well.'

He spoke as if Daisy's reaction was more important than Myrtle's death.

'I got to West Egg by a side road,' he continued, 'and left the car in my garage. I don't think anybody saw us, but I can't be sure.'

I disliked him so much at that moment that I didn't tell him he was wrong.

'Who was the woman?' he inquired.

'Her name was Wilson. Her husband owns the garage. How did it happen?'

'Well, I tried to turn the wheel –' he stopped, and suddenly I guessed the truth.

'Was Daisy driving?'

'Yes,' he said after a moment. 'But of course I'll say I was. When we left New York, she was very upset. She said she wanted to drive to calm herself down. Then this woman ran out onto the road just as we were passing a car that was coming the other way. It all happened in a minute. It seemed to me that the woman thought we were somebody she knew. She was waving her arms at us. I guess she was killed instantly.'

He paused.

'Daisy will be all right tomorrow,' he said. 'I'm going to wait here. She's locked herself into her room. If Tom tries to do anything violent she's going to turn the light off and on.'

GATSBY

★ What is Gatsby's reaction to the accident?
★ What does this tell us about him?

'He won't touch her,' I said. 'He's not thinking about her.'

'I don't trust him, old sport.'

A thought came to me just then. Suppose Tom found out that Daisy had been the driver. He might connect the two things in his mind.

'You wait here,' I said. 'I'll go and see if there's any sign of trouble.'

I walked back and looked in through the kitchen window. Daisy and Tom were sitting opposite each other at the table. He was talking to her. She looked up at him from time to time and nodded her head in agreement. There was an intimacy[1] between the people in front of me. Neither of them seemed happy or unhappy. They were like a couple who were planning something together.

'Is it all quiet?' asked Gatsby when I got back.

'Yes,' I replied. 'Why don't you come home and get some sleep?'

He shook his head.

'I'll wait here till Daisy goes to bed. Good night, old sport.'

I walked away and left him standing there in the moonlight, watching.

---

1 intimacy [ˈɪntəməsɪ] (n.) 親密

CHAPTER NINE

I couldn't sleep at all that night. Just before it got light I heard a taxi go up Gatsby's drive. I jumped out of bed, dressed and went over to his house.

The front door was open and he was in the hall. He looked tired.

'Nothing happened,' he said. 'I waited and at four o'clock she came to the window, stood there for a moment and then turned out the light.'

We went into the sitting room, opened the windows and sat smoking in the darkness.

'You should go away,' I said. 'They'll find your car.'

'Go away *now*, old sport?'

He didn't want to leave yet. He had to know what Daisy's plans were first. He was holding on to some last hope.

He told me about Dan Cody that night but he really wanted to talk about Daisy. He said she was the first 'nice girl'[1] he'd known. When she invited him to her house, he was amazed at how beautiful it was. Everything about it excited his imagination. He felt that it was full of romance and mystery, but he knew he didn't have the right to be there. He was poor and he had no past. The only things he had were his dreams and ambitions for a bright future. However, he let Daisy believe that he was from the same social class as her. He planned to take what he wanted from her and leave. He didn't expect to fall in love with her.

After the war he tried to get home, but he was sent to Oxford by mistake. Daisy's letters to him were full of despair[2]. Why couldn't he come home? She needed him to be there.

She needed to know that she was doing the right thing.

Daisy was beginning to feel the pressure of the world she lived in – an artificial world of orchids [3] and orchestras, of snobbery and hypocrisy [4]. She wanted her life to be decided immediately. That spring she met Tom Buchanan.

THE FUTURE

★ Have you made a plan for your future yet?
★ What would you like to do?
★ Where would you like to go?

'I don't think she ever loved him,' Gatsby said. 'He told her those things yesterday to frighten her, to make me look like a cheap [5] criminal. She didn't know what she was saying. Perhaps she loved him just for a minute when they were first married – and loved me more even then. Do you understand?'

It was nine o'clock and I had to go to work.

'I'll call you at noon,' I said.

'Do that, old sport,' he said. 'I suppose Daisy will call too.'

'I suppose so.'

'Well, goodbye.'

We shook hands. At the gate, I turned around and shouted, 'They're awful people. You're worth more than all of them put together.'

---

1 nice girl 在此指大家閨秀
2 despair [dɪˋspɛr] (n.) 絕望
3 orchid [ˋɔrkɪd] (n.) 蘭科植物
4 hypocrisy [hɪˋpɑkrəsɪ] (n.) 偽善；虛偽
5 cheap [tʃip] (a.) 在此指一無是處

🎧 I've always been glad I said that. It was the only compliment I ever gave him, because I disapproved of him from beginning to end.

I tried to do some work, but I fell asleep in my chair. Just before noon, the phone woke me. It was Jordan.

'I've left Daisy's house. I'm going to Southampton,' she said. 'You weren't very nice to me last night but I want to see you again.'

'I want to see you, too.'

'Suppose I don't go to Southampton, and come into town this afternoon!'

'No – not this afternoon.'

We talked for a while and the call ended because one of us put the receiver down. I don't know which. I just knew that I didn't want to talk to her any more that day.

I called Gatsby's house four times, but they told me the line was busy.

Now I want to go back a little and explain what happened at the garage after we left there the night before.

Michaelis stayed with Wilson after the accident. Wilson was confused, but about three o'clock in the morning he began to talk about the yellow car. He said he had a way of finding out who it belonged[1] to. He also said that two months ago his wife had come home with a broken nose and bruises[2] on her face.

'Then he killed her,' said Wilson.

'Who killed her?'

'I have a way of finding out.'

'It was an accident, George.'

'It was the man in that car,' Wilson said with conviction[3]. 'She ran out to speak to him and he didn't stop.'

WILSON

★ How is Wilson going to find out who the yellow car belongs to?
★ What is he going to do when he knows?

At six o'clock Michaelis left Wilson. When he returned to the garage at ten, Wilson wasn't there. The police guessed he had spent the morning looking for the owner of the yellow car. At half-past two he was in West Egg, where he asked someone the way to Gatsby's house.

---

1 belong [bəˈlɔŋ] (v.) 屬於
2 bruise [bruz] (n.) 青腫；瘀傷
3 conviction [kənˈvɪkʃən] (n.) 堅信

Gatsby put on his bathing suit[1] at two o'clock. He told his butler to come and tell him if anyone phoned. Before going to his swimming pool, he went to his garage and picked up a water mattress[2].

No telephone messages came.

The chauffeur heard the shots[3] but didn't go to investigate. He said later that he hadn't thought they were very important.

When I got to the station that evening, I drove straight to Gatsby's house. I think everyone in the house knew what had happened but they didn't say anything. In complete silence, the chauffeur, butler, gardener and I hurried down to the pool. The wind was making small ripples[4] on the surface of the water and moving the mattress and its burden[5] slowly towards the edge of the pool.

As we were carrying Gatsby's body back to the house, we saw Wilson's body. It was lying in the grass not far from the pool.

1 bathing suit 泳衣
2 water mattress 充氣浮板
3 shot [ʃɑt] (n.) 槍聲
4 ripple ['rɪpl] (n.) 漣漪
5 burden ['bɝdn̩] (n.) 負擔；重擔

THINK

★ Was Gatsby expecting to be killed?
★ Who killed Wilson?

CHAPTER TEN

During the rest of that day and the next, there was a continuous coming and going of policemen, photographers and newspaper men.

At the inquest[1] Michaelis mentioned that Wilson suspected his wife of having a lover. Myrtle's sister Catherine swore Myrtle had never seen Gatsby and was completely happy with her husband. Wilson was called a man 'deranged[2] by grief[3]' and the case[4] ended there.

I informed West Egg village of the catastrophe[5] and from that moment on everything was referred to me. I became responsible for all the practical details because nobody else was interested.

I had phoned Daisy half an hour after we found him, but she and Tom had already left.

Next morning I sent a letter to Wolfsheim. I asked him to come on the next train. He replied saying that he was too busy and didn't want to be involved. A more tender feeling for Gatsby started to grow inside me.

On the third day a telegram arrived from Minnesota. It was signed Henry C. Gatz and said he was leaving immediately. He wanted to be at the funeral and asked us to wait for him.

Gatsby's father was an old man with a sad face. He was wearing a long, warm coat although it was only September. He was obviously exhausted[6] so I took him to the music room and asked the butler to bring him a glass of milk.

'I saw it in the Chicago newspaper,' he said.

'I didn't know how to contact you.'

'Where is Jimmy?'

I pointed to the sitting room.

He got up slowly and went into the room where his son lay. After a little while he came out, his eyes full of tears.

'He had a big future. He was young but he had a lot of brain power.'

'That's true,' I said, uncomfortably.

NICK

★ Imagine you are Nick.
★ What are you thinking at this moment?
★ Why do you have 'a more tender feeling' for Gatsby now?
★ Will you stay in West Egg?

The morning of the funeral I went to see Meyer Wolfsheim.

'You were his closest friend,' I said, 'so I know you'll want to come to his funeral.'

'I'd like to,' he said, 'but I can't do it. When a man gets killed, I keep out. I used to be different but now – '

I got back to West Egg and went next door to see Mr Gatz.

'Had you seen him recently?' I asked.

'He came to me two years ago and bought me the house I live in. We were very upset when he ran away from home, but I see there was a reason for it. He knew he had a big future. And after his success he was very generous with me.'

A little before three o'clock, a Lutheran[7] priest arrived. We waited and watched for half an hour but nobody else came.

---

1 inquest [ˈɪnˌkwɛst] (n.) 審問
2 derange [dɪˈrendʒ] (v.) 發狂
3 grief [grif] (n.) 悲痛;悲傷
4 case [kes] (n.) 案子
5 catastrophe [kəˈtæstrəfɪ] (n.) 災禍
6 exhausted [ɪgˈzɔstɪd] (a.) 疲憊不堪的
7 Lutheran [ˈluθərən] (a.) 路德教派的

It was raining when we got to the cemetery[1]. Mr Gatz, the minister and I were in the limousine, and a little later four or five servants and the postman from West Egg arrived in Gatsby's station wagon. Then another car arrived. It was a man I'd met once in Gatsby's library.

I tried to think about Gatsby, but he was already too far away. I could only remember that Daisy hadn't sent a message or flowers.

After the service we went quickly through the rain to our cars.

'I couldn't get to the house,' the man from Gatsby's library said.

'Nobody could.'

'But hundreds of people used to go there before,' he said. 'The poor man.'

After Gatsby's death the East wasn't the same for me, so I decided to leave.

I saw Jordan Baker before I left and talked over what had happened to us, and what had happened afterwards to me. When I'd finished she told me that she was engaged to another man. I didn't believe her, but I pretended to be surprised. For a minute I thought that I was making a mistake. Then I stood up and said goodbye. I was angry, half in love with her and very sorry.

---

1 cemetery [ˈsɛməˌtɛrɪ] (n.) 墓地

One afternoon in October I saw Tom. He was walking along Fifth Avenue. He saw me and held out his hand. I didn't take it.

'What's the matter, Nick? Do you object to shaking hands with me?'

'Yes. You know what I think of you.'

'You're crazy, Nick,' he said quickly.

'What did you say to Wilson that afternoon?' I asked. I suspected Wilson had gone to see him before going to Gatsby's place.

He stared at me silently, and I knew the answer.

I started to turn away, but he held my arm.

'I told him the truth,' he said. 'He came to the door and tried to force his way upstairs. He was crazy. His hand was on his gun. He wanted to know who owned the car. He was ready to kill me. I had to tell him, but Gatsby deserved[1] it. He deceived you just like he did Daisy. He was an insensitive man. He ran over[2] Myrtle and never even stopped his car.'

There was nothing I could say, except that it wasn't true. I couldn't forgive him or like him, but I saw that what he had done was, to him, correct. I shook hands with him. It seemed silly not to because I suddenly felt that I was talking to a child, not a grown man.

On my last night in West Egg, I went and looked at Gatsby's empty house. I walked onto his beach. Most of the big houses were closed for the winter now. I thought about Gatsby. I remembered the time when he had stretched out his arms to the green light at the end of Daisy's dock. His dream probably seemed so close that he couldn't fail to get hold of it. He did not know that it was already behind him.

---

1 deserve [dɪ`zɝv] (v.) 應受；該得
2 run over 輾過

AFTER READING

Ⓐ Personal Response

1 Work with a partner. Discuss what you liked most and least about this story.

2 Did this story remind you of any films or TV series you have seen, or stories you have read? If so, tell your partner.

3 Do you think this story could happen today? Why/ why not? What changes, if any, would there be?

4 "*The Great Gatsby* is a beautiful love story." Discuss this idea in a group of four.

5 Is there anything that you would like to change in the story? Can you think of any way to improve the story?

6 Do you think the story has a moral, and if so, what is it?

❸ Comprehension

7 Tick (✓) true (T) or false (F) below.

T F   (a) Jay Gatsby comes from a very rich family.
T F   (b) The Buchanans have a three-year-old daughter.
T F   (c) Gatsby and Daisy don't hide their love for each other.
T F   (d) Nick Carraway gets engaged to Jordan Baker.
T F   (e) George and Myrtle Wilson have a happy marriage.
T F   (f) Myrtle Wilson is not Tom Buchanan's first mistress.
T F   (g) Gatsby is driving when Myrtle is killed.
T F   (h) Gatsby kills Wilson in the garden.

8 Complete the sentences with the words in the box.

> sister   father   business partner
> second cousin   husband   neighbor

(a) Jay Gatsby is Nick Carraway's _____.
(b) Daisy is Nick's _____.
(c) Meyer Wolfsheim is Gatsby's _____.
(d) Catherine is Myrtle Wilson's _____.
(e) Tom is Daisy's _____.
(f) Henry C. Gatz is Gatsby's _____.

9 Put these sentences from the story in the right order.

_1_   ⓐ I decided to go to New York to work in the finance business.

_____   ⓑ She was telling him she loved him with her eyes.

_____   ⓒ We went to a restaurant on Forty-second Street, where Gatsby introduced me to his friend Wolfsheim.

_____   ⓓ So Tom Buchanan, his girl and I went to New York.

_____   ⓔ Daisy and Gatsby danced.

_____   ⓕ After Gatsby's death the East wasn't the same for me, so I decided to leave.

_____   ⓖ He was standing with his arms stretching out towards the water.

_____   ⓗ I rang Daisy the next morning and asked her to come to tea.

10 Work with a partner. Read these things that Nick says in the story and discuss the questions.

ⓐ "My father runs a hardware business that has been in the family since 1851."
↳ Why did Nick decide not to work with his father in the family hardware business when he finished university?

ⓑ "Anyway I drove to East Egg to see two people that I didn't really know very well."
↳ Why did he decide to do that? What did he expect to happen?

ⓒ "I have always been an honest person and I knew I couldn't continue to deceive her."
↳ Who is 'her' in this sentence? How was Nick deceiving this woman?

ⓓ "Not for the first time, I changed my opinion of him."
↳ Who is 'him' in this sentence? Why did Nick change his opinion of this man so often?

ⓒ Characters

11 Who are the characters in the descriptions?

    ⓐ Her face was sad and lovely, with bright eyes and a passionate mouth.

    ⓑ She was a slim girl, who stood very straight. Her grey eyes looked out of a pale, discontented face.

    ⓒ He was a strong man of thirty. He was arrogant and seemed aggressive. His body was muscular and powerful.

    ⓓ She was in her mid-thirties. She wasn't beautiful and she was a little plump but there was life and energy in her body.

    ⓔ She was a slim girl of thirty, with red hair and a pale face.

    ⓕ He didn't look like a sinister person with his attractive, tanned face and short, tidy hair.

12 Which of the main characters in the book do you like most and which one least? Explain your reasons to a partner.

13 How do these characters' change their behavior in the story? How is the change described and shown?

    ⓐ George B. Wilson, after he finds out about Myrtle's affair.
    ⓑ Tom Buchanan, after the road accident.

Discuss your answers in a group of four.

14 Who says these things? Who do they say them to? Why do they say them?

ⓐ Don't believe everything you hear, Nick.

ⓑ This is an unusual party for me. I haven't seen the host.

ⓒ He's the man who fixed the World Series in 1919.

ⓓ Let's go to Coney Island, old sport, in my car.

ⓔ I've been here too long. My wife and I want to go West.

ⓕ Even alone I can't say I never loved Tom.

 15 Read about Francis Scott Fitzgerald on pages 4-7 and check on the Internet. Make a list of the similarities between the events in Fitzgerald's own life and the events in the story.

🅓 Plot and Theme

🔊 **16** Work in groups of four, and discuss the following statements. Which ones best reflect the themes of the story?

- a Life is no good if you aren't rich and famous.
- b You should never try to be something you aren't.
- c Money cannot buy love.
- d True love always wins in the end.

🔊 **17** Think about historical characters who have had the word *great* attached to their name (e.g. Alexander the Great, King Alfred the Great, Peter the Great). What does it mean about them? Is Gatsby really 'Great'? If so, in what way? If not, why not, and why did Fitzgerald give the book this title? Discuss with a partner. Think of alternative titles for the book.

18 Nick Carraway is the narrator, but he is also a character in the story. How does this affect what we know about the events of the story?

19 Tom Buchanan finds out that Gatsby made his fortune through crime – probably selling alcohol illegally ('bootlegging'). Did you feel any differently about Gatsby when you found out he was a criminal?

🔊 Discuss your ideas in groups of four.

20 Discuss how each of the following characters tries to achieve his or her version of the American Dream. What advice would you give each one?

	How he/she tried to achieve his/her dream	Your Advice

21 What do you think Nick does when he goes back to the West at the end of the novel? Imagine you are Nick. Write a letter of 100-120 words to Jordan Baker a year later, saying what has happened to you in the last twelve months. Give your letter to a partner and ask him/her to reply.

E Language

22 Look at this sentence from the story:

"During dinner, Daisy and Miss Baker talked in a way that was as cool as their white dresses."

The structure as cool as their white dresses is called a simile. A simile is the comparison of two unlike things using the words 'as' or 'like'. Complete these similes with ideas of your own.

a The sand on the beach was as hot as
   _____ and burnt our feet.

b Angela has black hair and her eyes are as blue as
   _____.

c Jane isn't a very good cook. Instead of being light and soft, her cakes are always like _____.

d I couldn't understand the newsreader. He spoke as fast as
   _____.

e I've been working in the garden all day and I'm as tired as
   _____.

f Silvia has a beautiful voice. She sings like
   _____.

Share your sentences with the class. Vote for the most interesting similes.

23 Complete the sentences from the story with the prepositions in the box.

> inside   off   under   in   on
> out   to   from   over   up

a   Tom stopped impatiently _____ Wilson's sign.

b   Tom frowned, and without a word went _____ .

c   I looked _____ to sea but I could only see a green light.

d   And she hurried _____ to join her group, who were waiting for her at the door.

e   Something very sad happened _____ me long ago.

f   He planned to take what he wanted _____ her and leave.

g   In the west there were pink and golden clouds _____ the sea.

h   Tom picked Wilson _____ and carried him into the office.

i   She looked up at him from time to time and nodded her head _____ agreement.

j   The wind was making small ripples _____ the surface of the water.

24 Read these phrases about homes from the story

a   a red and white <u>mansion</u> with a lawn that stretched all the way down to the beach

b   Myrtle will be hurt if you don't come to the <u>apartment</u>.

c   Young men didn't arrive from nowhere to buy a <u>palace</u> on Long Island Sound.

d   I want you and Daisy to come to my <u>house</u>.

Work with a partner. Make a list of the differences between these four types of home.

TEST

1 Listen and tick (✓) the correct picture.

2 Tick (✓) true (T) or false (F).

T F	a	Tom and Nick were at Yale University together.
T F	b	Jordan and Daisy grew up in the same town.
T F	c	Gatsby sent Nick an invitation to one of his parties.
T F	d	Nick and Jordan fell in love.
T F	e	Jordan didn't believe that Gatsby had studied at Oxford University.
T F	f	Gatsby was anxious about seeing Daisy again.
T F	g	After the tea party, Gatsby told Nick the truth about his past.
T F	h	Tom admired Gatsby because he was a self-made man.
T F	i	Daisy often visited Gatsby in his mansion.
T F	j	Wilson wanted to leave the East because Myrtle was ill.
T F	k	In the hotel room, Daisy confessed that she had never loved Tom.
T F	l	Myrtle was waving at her Greek neighbor when she was hit by the car.
T F	m	After the accident, Gatsby went to the Buchanan's house to talk to Tom.
T F	n	Wilson spent all of the following morning looking for the yellow car.
T F	o	Daisy asked Nick to take care of the funeral arrangements and then left.
T F	p	Nick wrote to Gatsby's father to tell him what had happened.

Changing the Narrator

The Great Gatsby is narrated by Nick Carraway,
and so we see everything from his point of view.
For example, there is no information about what
Gatsby did in West Egg before Nick arrived there,
nothing about the things he did on his own when
Nick wasn't around, about his business deals, apart
from the little Nick overhears, and so on. This is
what happens in story writing when we have a
single narrator.

Work with a partner, and tell the story from
the point of view of either Jay Gatsby or Daisy
Buchanan. Think about these things:

1. *How and when did you come to West Egg (Gatsby) or East Egg (Daisy) and why?*
2. *How did you spend your time before Nick Carraway arrived there?*
3. *Explain your feelings about Gatsby/Daisy.*
4. *Say how you felt about the first meeting with Gatsby/ Daisy, the meeting in the Plaza Hotel room and the car accident.*
5. *Daisy, say how you felt about Gatsby's death, where you went and what you think your future will be.*

Write scenes from the story, making sure you write it in the first person ("I" meaning either Gatsby or Daisy), and expressing your feelings and opinions about things.

作者簡介 弗朗西斯‧費茲傑羅，於 1896 年出生於美國明尼蘇達州的聖保羅市，他出身上層中產階級家庭，而且是一個信仰天主教的愛爾蘭家庭。 1913 年，他進入名校普林斯頓大學就讀。他在大學期間寫了第一本小說，但沒有出版社願意幫他出書。五年之後，他輟學入伍。

1919 年，他邂逅了年僅十七歲的美麗女孩潔塔‧塞爾，他有意娶她進門，但她愛慕虛榮，而且只喜歡玩樂。為了滿足她的需求，他退伍並搬到紐約找工作。

1920 年，他出版了小說《塵世樂園》（This Side of Paradise），成為文壇一顆閃亮的新星。他現在的收入讓潔塔願意點頭嫁給他，他們開始過著奢華的生活，參加各種聚會和社交活動，並在美國和歐洲各處遊歷。

他的第二本小說《美麗與毀滅》（The Beautiful and Damned，1922 年出版）和第三本小說《大亨小傳》（1925 年出版）不如首部小說那樣大賣，便常常舉債度日。1930 年，潔塔精神分裂，並於 1932 年住進精神療養院，一直成為他的經濟負擔。

1937 年，他前往好萊塢，擔任編劇的工作。他有酗酒的問題，健康每下愈況。1940 年，因心臟病發病逝。

本書簡介 費茲傑羅早期生活的一些經驗，出現在他最有名的小說《大亨小傳》裡。《大亨小傳》是他的第三本小說，於 1925 年出版，時值爵士年代的中期。這本小說被喻為「美國第一本現代小說」，因為其所描繪的是第一次世界大戰到 1930 年代華爾街股災期間的社會現象。小說以一則愛情故事為主軸，卻也傳達出「美國夢」的結束。

小說中的故事場景設定在東岸的紐約市，而故事的主要人物——傑‧蓋茨比、倪克‧賈若維、卜江南夫婦湯姆和黛希——這些人都來自美國的中西部鄉下。

蓋茨比代表了美國新興的富豪。他白手起家，即使故事暗示了他可能是因為從事非法勾當而致富。湯姆‧卜江南代表的是美國家財萬貫的權貴家庭。這兩個人同樣過著奢華的生活，他們開跑車，到處旅行，住在豪宅裡，穿著名貴。

故事中第一人稱的敘事者倪克，並不是湯姆或蓋茨比社交圈裡的朋友，只因為他是蓋茨比的鄰居、湯姆妻子的表親，才和他們攀上關係。一開始，他們的世界讓倪克覺得很新鮮，但到了最後，他厭倦了環繞在蓋茨比身邊的人，因為在東岸富裕的生活下，是一片空虛和不道德的生活。最後，他決定搬回中西部。

《大亨小傳》曾多次被改編成電影，其中最有名的是 1974 年拍成的版本，由勞勃‧瑞福和米亞‧法羅主演。

CHAPTER ONE

P.13

在我們這個中西部城市，賈若維家族三代以來都是地方上的望族。我父親繼承從一八五一年就開始經營的五金行生意。

我一九一五年從耶魯大學畢業之後，從戎參加了第一次世界大戰。退役後，我決定去紐約的金融業工作，這是一九二二年的事。

我在長島租了一間不起眼的小房子。長島上有兩個卵形的半島，隔著長島海灣，我就住在西半島「西雅歌」的邊陲。西半島沒那麼時尚，我住的地方離海邊只有五十公尺遠。我的房子夾在兩棟大房子的中間，大房子的租金一年要一萬五千元。在我右邊的大宅院特別漂亮，有一座四十畝大的花園，那是蓋茨比公館。

有一天晚上，我去卜江南家吃飯，這個夏天的故事就從這裡開始。黛希是我的遠房表妹，湯姆是我在大學時代的同學。湯姆喜歡運動的，他在耶魯時打過橄欖球隊。他家道殷實，他們夫妻在法國旅居過一年，之後又四海為家，往來的都是

富貴人家。黛希在電話上跟我說，他們這次準備落腳定居了，但我不太相信，因為湯姆不是那種可以長久待在某個地方的人。

P.14

我開車前往東雅歌，去拜訪這兩個我猜不太透的人。他們的房子比我想像得還氣派，那是一棟紅白相間的大廈，大草坪一路延伸到海灘邊。

久別重逢，湯姆的樣子都變了。他現在看起來酷酷的，有點目中無人的樣子。他獵裝下的肌肉又大塊又結實，給人一種招惹不起的感覺。

我們在陽台小敘了一下，然後才進到屋內，這時沙發上已經坐了兩位年輕的女士。黛希起身迎接我，而比較年輕的那位女郎，我並不認識。黛希拉起我的手，盯著我的臉打量著。

「看到你，我真是太高興了！」她說。

黛希說，另外那個女子姓貝克，現在住在他們家。黛希的臉龐略帶憂鬱而甜美，她有一雙水汪汪的眼睛和一對豐厚的嘴唇。

「你一定要看看小寶寶。」黛希說。

「好呀！」

「她現在睡著了。她今年三歲了。」

「倪克，你現在在做什麼？」湯姆問。

「我在金融界工作。」

「哪家銀行？」

我回答了湯姆。

湯姆回道：「沒聽過。」

「你在東部待久一點就會聽過了。」我說。

「我是會留在東部，傻瓜才會離開這

裡。」湯姆一邊説，一邊看了一下黛希。

P.15

貝克小姐接話道：「沒錯！」

這是我進門後貝克小姐第一次出聲。我看著她，她很纖瘦，站得很挺。她用灰色的眸子看著我，她的臉蛋白皙而迷人，但帶著一種不滿的表情。我覺得她看起來似曾相識。

「你住在西雅歌，對吧？我那裡有認識的人。」她説。

「真的？我還沒有認識的人呢。」

「你一定聽過蓋茨比吧？」

「蓋茨比？誰是蓋茨比？」黛希問。

我還沒回答蓋茨比就住在我隔壁時，就有人來叫我們吃飯了。我們隨即進到了陽臺。

飯席間，黛希和貝克小姐的交談冷淡，就和她們身上穿的夏裝一樣淡漠。

「黛希，你讓我覺得自己很不文明，你能不能聊聊農作物或是談點別的嗎？」我後來説道。

這時，電話響起，男管家去接了電話。一會兒後他走回來，在湯姆的耳邊説了幾句話。湯姆眉頭一皺，一言不發地走進屋內。黛希把餐巾擱在桌上，也跟著進了屋子。

我正要開口時，貝克小姐跟我「噓」了一下。

隔壁房間傳來一陣低聲而激動的交談聲，貝克小姐傾身豎耳偷聽。

「你提到的蓋茨比先生，他就住在我隔壁……」我説。

「你先別説話，我想聽聽看發生了什麼事。」

「是發生了什麼事情嗎？」我不知情地問。

P.16

貝克小姐訝異地説：「你不知道嗎？湯姆在紐約有外遇。」

「外遇？」我重複她的話説。

「在晚餐時間來電，這女人太不識相了！」

我還沒弄明白她的意思，湯姆和黛希這時就回到了餐桌上。

晚餐結束後，貝克小姐和湯姆走進書房，我則跟著黛希走到陽台。我們並排坐下，聊了一下她女兒。

「倪克，雖然我們是表親，但我們也不是太熟。是這樣的，我過得很不好，一團亂，大家都這麼覺得，我知道。我也到處走遍、看遍、玩遍了。」

她的眼底閃閃有光。

「我是這麼的世故。」她一邊説，一邊哈哈地苦笑著。

我不太相信她的話，她沒有説出真心話，我覺得不是很自在。

我們接著去書房找湯姆和貝克小姐。當我們一走進去時，貝克小姐就站起來説：「十點了，該睡了。」

「瓊玥明天還要打高爾夫比賽。」黛希解釋道。

「哦，你是瓊玥・貝克？」我問。

難怪我覺得她似曾相識。

「晚安，明天早上八點把我搖醒好嗎？晚安，賈若維先生，改天見。」

「當然啦。倪克，你要常過來，我想你們可以多認識一下彼此。」黛希語氣堅定地説。

P. 18

瓊玥離開後，湯姆説：「她是個好女生。」

「她是紐約人嗎？」我問。

「她是陸宜市人，我們從小一塊兒長大的。」黛希説。

「你和倪克在陽臺上有聊心事嗎？」湯姆突然問道。

「有嗎？我不記得了。」黛希説。

「倪克，別聽到什麼都信以為真。」湯姆告誡我説。

在我準備告辭時，黛希説：「倪克！我忘了問你一件重要的事，聽説你在西部和一位女孩訂了婚。」

「我現在事業無成，還談不到結婚。」我回答。

我知道黛希為什麼這麼問，有人謠傳説我訂婚了，這些流言蜚語也正是我搬來東部的一個原因。

我開車走在回家的路上，心裡感到納悶，甚至還有點反感。我覺得黛希應該帶著寶寶離開，但她好像沒有這個打算。而湯姆在紐約有女人，這倒不是太意外。

湯姆・卜江南這個人

• 倪克説，湯姆看起來「酷酷的，有點目中無人的樣子」。湯姆有哪些行為舉止，讓倪克產生這種感覺？

P. 19

夏夜迷人，我回到家時，在花園裡坐了一會兒。我看到那邊有一個身影在移動，我並不是一個人，鄰居也正待在他的花園裡。他站在那裡，雙手對著海水伸出去。我朝大海望了望，只看到豆大的綠光，那裡大概是碼頭的盡頭。等我再把頭轉回去時，蓋茨比先生的人已經不見了。黑暗中，獨留我一人。

CHAPTER TWO

P. 20

星期天下午，我和湯姆搭地鐵前往紐約。地鐵在吊橋前停了一下，讓船隻先行通過。這時，湯姆突然跳了起來。

「我們在這裡下車，我讓你見見我的情婦。」湯姆説。

我們跳下車，往回走了一百公尺左右，來到了一個小小的住宅區。住宅區裡有三家商店，其中有一家是修車行。湯姆走進修車行，我跟了進去。裡頭很簡陋，什麼東西都沒有。這時出現了一位臉色蒼白的金髮男人。

「哈囉，魏爾森，生意還好嗎？」湯姆問。

「還過得去。你什麼時候才要把那輛車賣給我？」魏爾森問。

「下個星期吧，我手下的人還在修理。」

這時，走出來了一位三十五歲左右的女子。她長得不特別漂亮，身材略為豐滿，渾身散發著活力和熱情。她走過丈夫的身旁，朝著湯姆走過來，臉上慢慢堆起笑容。她跟湯姆握了握手，兩人四目相對。

「還不拿椅子過來給我們坐！」她頭也沒轉地對丈夫說。

「說得對！」

魏爾森一往辦公間走去，妻子就將身體挨近湯姆。

「我想見你，你搭下一班地鐵。」湯姆柔情地說。

她點了點頭，從他身邊走開，這時魏爾森搬了兩張椅子過來。

P.22

隨後，我們在公路上沒人看見的地方等她。

「很恐怖的地方，對吧？」湯姆說。

「是沒錯。」

「換換環境對她有好處。」

「她丈夫沒意見嗎？」

「你說魏爾森？他以為她是去找妹妹，他不是很聰明。」

就這樣，湯姆・卜江南和他的情婦，我們三個人一起前往紐約。我們在車站招了一輛計程車。

我們來到第五大道時，我說：「我就在這裡下了。」

「你別走啊，如果你不跟我們上去公寓坐坐，茉桃（譯註：即魏爾森太太）會生氣的，對不對，茉桃？」

「對啊，我打電話叫我妹妹凱薩琳過來，大家都說她長得很漂亮。」茉桃懇求道。

車子在一五八號街停了下來。

「我再把馬基夫婦請過來。」茉桃說道。

茉桃的妹妹年紀三十上下，身材很苗條，有著一頭紅色的頭髮，臉色白皙。馬基先生就住在樓下，他皮膚很白，有點陰柔，是個攝影師。他有一個讓人招架不住的老婆，他老婆得意洋洋地告訴我，她丈夫已經為她拍了一百二十七張照片！

凱薩琳坐在我旁邊，她問我說：「你住在長島嗎？」

「我住在西雅歌。」

「我一個月前才去那裡參加過一場派對，在一個姓蓋茨比的人的家裡。你認識他嗎？」

「我就住在他隔壁。」

「聽說他是德國威廉皇帝的侄子，所以才那麼有錢。」

P.23

「我想去長島拍照做生意，但缺人牽線。」馬基先生說。

「你可以請茉桃幫你牽線。」湯姆說罷，逕自哈哈大笑。

這時，魏爾森太太正好端著托盤走進來。「茉桃，你可以幫馬基先生寫封推薦信給你丈夫，讓他去幫你丈夫拍幾張相片。」

凱薩琳湊到我耳邊，小聲地跟我說：「他們兩個都受不了自己的那口子，我想他們乾脆各自離一離，然後兩個人再結婚算了。」

我用訝異的表情看著凱薩琳。

「湯姆的老婆不願意成全他們，他老婆是天主教徒，不肯離婚。」

黛希並不是天主教徒，我對這個謊言有點震驚。

說謊

- 湯姆為什麼要對茉桃說他的妻子是天主教徒？
- 你想一個人會說謊，可能會有哪些原因？
- 說謊的行為一定是不好的嗎？

「等他們結婚了，他們準備到西部去住一陣子，等到風波過去再回來。」凱薩琳接著說。

「我也差一點嫁了一個門不當、戶不對的男人。」馬基太太突然說。

「但你終究沒有嫁給他，而我是真的嫁了。」茉桃說。

「她實在應該離開他。」凱薩琳又在我耳邊說。

P.24

我們開了第二瓶威士忌。馬基先生睡著了。我想去公園走走，但每次我起身告辭時，就會被捲入一陣爭論中，沒能走得開。

快到半夜的時候，我聽到湯姆和魏爾森太太在討論說，魏爾森太太是否有資格提黛希這個名字。

「黛希！黛希！我什麼時候想叫，我就叫！」魏爾森太太喊道。

湯姆‧卜江南一個巴掌往她的臉上呼過去，她立刻流下了鼻血。

我拿起我的帽子，轉身離開。

我只記得我後來眯眯矇矇地躺在賓州車站裡，等候清早四點鐘的火車。

CHAPTER THREE

P.25

蓋茨比家幾乎夜夜笙歌，賓客絡繹不絕。午後時光，他的訪客們會在海邊游泳，或是在沙灘上做日光浴，他的兩艘汽艇會在海灘飆船。他的那輛勞斯萊斯像是公車一樣，不斷地往返城裡接送客人，他的旅車會去地鐵站接所有的班車。每到星期一，就要動用到八名僕人來清理週末所留下的殘局。

外燴人員會固定帶彩色燈泡來布置花園，他們會架起桌子，在桌子上擺滿冷盤、各種沙拉和派餅。他們也在屋

子裡設了一個酒吧。樂隊會在七點的時候到達，這時游泳的客人已經從海灘回來，正忙著換晚禮服。陸續還有更多客人坐著自家的車子抵達，宴會很快如火如荼地展開。

我想我第一次前往蓋茨比家，是少數真正在應邀名單中的客人。他們這些客人大都是不請自來，而蓋茨比是當天早上派人送請柬來給我，上面寫著：如蒙光臨宴會，不勝榮幸。

我剛進去蓋茨比家時，很不自在，因為我一個人也不認識。我尋找蓋茨比先生的身影，但沒有人知道他在哪裡。我站在酒吧邊，想灌些酒來讓自己自在些，而就是這時，瓊玟．貝克走進了花園。

「哈囉！」我喊道。

「我猜你可能會在這裡，我記得你說你就住在隔壁。」她說。

P.27

這時，有兩位身穿黃色禮服的女子從旁邊走過。

「哈囉！你沒有贏得比賽，真可惜啊！」她們喊道。

瓊玟在上星期的高爾夫決賽中不幸落敗。

我們在花園中信步了一會兒，接著在吧檯點了雞尾酒。我們在一張桌子旁坐下，同桌的還有那兩位黃衣女子和三位男士。

「這裡的派對你常來嗎？」瓊玟問坐在旁邊

的女子。

「我常來啊！我上一次還站在椅子上把我的衣服給撕破了，蓋茨比就跟我要了姓名和住址，一個星期之後，我收到一個包裹，裡面是一件新的晚禮服。你們一定猜不到，他竟然花了二百六十五塊錢買一件洋裝！」

「這種人竟然會做這種事，真是稀奇！他一向不想跟任何人有瓜葛。」另一個女子說。

「你是指誰？」我問。

「蓋茨比啊，有人跟我說，他殺過人！」

「這不知道是真的假的，不過他在大戰期間擔任過德國間諜。」另一個女子說。

「這我也聽說過，是一個從小和他在德國一起長大的人跟我說的。」一位男士說。

「不會吧！他大戰期間是待在美國軍隊裡的。」第一個女子說。

人們隨著樂隊的音樂娑婆起舞。隨後一個男高音獻唱了一首義大利歌曲，接著一杯杯香檳酒被端了上來。我和瓊玟走進屋裡想找尋主人，但一無所獲。我們又點了杯酒，在一張桌子旁坐下，旁邊還有一位男士和一位女子。男士的年齡和我相仿，女子則是動不動就忍不住放聲大笑。我這時候已經比較放得開了。

在娛樂節目中途休息時間，那位男士看著我，對我笑了笑。

「您看起來很面善，您大戰期間不是被編在第一師？」男子很有禮貌地問。

「對，我是。」

「我也是在第一師，我就覺得你眼熟！」

我們聊到了法國。他又跟我說，他剛買了一艘新船，明天早上要出海試試。

「你要不要一起去，弟兄？」

「幾點？」

「都可以，你方便就好。」

我轉過頭對這位新朋友說：「這個派對對我來說有點奇怪，我連主人的面都沒見著。我就住在那邊，蓋茨比給我送了請帖。」我指著我的房子說。

他用詫異的眼神看著我。

「我就是蓋茨比啊！」他說。

「什麼！噢，真對不起。」我喊道。

「弟兄，我還以為你知道呢！看來我不是個盡職的主人。」

這時，一位男管家走過來跟蓋茨比先生說，有芝加哥來的電話要找他。

「弟兄，抱歉啦，待會見。」他說。

派對

• 你喜歡參加派對嗎？
• 你辦過派對嗎？

我還以為蓋茨比先生應該是一位長得福福態態、紅光滿面的中年人。

我轉身問瓊玥說：「他是何方神聖？」

「不就一個姓蓋茨比的男人嘛。」

「我是說他是哪裡人？是幹什麼的？」

「現在你也問起這件事啦。」瓊玥笑著說：「他跟我說過，他上過牛津大學，不過我不大相信。」

她的話，讓我想到另一個女子所說的「他殺過人」。我起了好奇心。不可能隨隨便便冒出一個年輕人，就能在長島買下豪宅。

傑・蓋茨比

• 蓋茨比的過去為什麼顯得這麼神祕？
• 他的財富是從哪裡來的？

樂隊奏起了爵士樂。我環顧四周，看到蓋茨比正站在房子的臺階上，很滿意地看著每個人。他留著一頭整潔的短髮，皮膚曬得黑黑的，長得很有魅力，怎麼也不像是個罪惡之徒。

「貝克小姐，打擾您了，蓋茨比先生想單獨跟您說說話。」蓋茨比的男管家說。

「跟我？」她喊道。

「是的，小姐。」

她站起身來，驚訝地望著我，然後跟著管家離開。

我一個人待在那裡，時間已經快兩點了。這時，露台上方的一間房間裡傳來一陣鬧哄哄的聲音。我走進房間，看到裡頭擠滿了人。穿黃色洋裝的其中一位女子正在彈鋼琴，有一位來自知名合唱團的紅髮女子正在高歌。

到了曲終人散的時刻，我準備打道回府。我走進大廳，取我的帽子。這時，書房的房門打開，裡頭走出來了瓊玥和蓋茨比。

瓊玥在我耳邊小聲說：「我剛剛聽到了一個驚人的消息，不過我發誓我不會說出去。」她打了個哈欠，又說：「你要來找我喔！」

她隨即去找她的朋友，他們在一旁待著。

我走到蓋茨比身旁的人群裡。我想跟他說我下午就在找他了，也想跟他道個歉，說我在花園裡時沒有認出他來。

P.31

「弟兄，這不需要放在心上！」他一邊說，一邊把手搭在我肩上。他的言談舉止友善而真誠，但我感受不到他真正的情感。

朋友

- 倪克會和蓋茨比成為好朋友嗎？
- 要成為一位好朋友，最重要的因素應該是什麼？
- 你如何當別人的好朋友？

「別忘了我們明天要搭新船出海。我九點去接你。」他說。

這時，管男家說：「先生，有一通費城來的電話要找您。」

「跟他說我這就來。晚安了，弟兄！」

「晚安。」

我穿過草坪走回家。我佇足，回首望了一眼，天上有一眉新月，月光灑在蓋茨比的宅邸上。夜色清朗，我想起了當晚的音樂和笑聲。花園裡的燈光還亮著，但房子裡已經客去樓空。

P.32

以上這些，是我在那年夏天的三個派對夜晚所留意到的事。不過我這樣講並不忠實，因為這三個夜晚隔了幾個星期，而這期間我的生活忙得不可開交。我大部分時間都在紐約工作，我和辦公室的其他年輕同事來往，和他們在人潮擁擠的餐廳裡一起吃午餐，我還和會計處的一位女子有過短暫的邂逅。後來我趁她度假之際，讓這段韻事悄悄而逝。

我大都在耶魯俱樂部吃晚餐，然後上樓去圖書室看書，消磨個一個鐘頭。接著，我會沿著麥迪遜大道走，穿過三十三號街走到賓州車站。我開始喜歡上紐約的生活。

我有一陣子沒見到瓊玥‧貝克，一直到仲夏時才又遇見她。一開始，我喜歡跟她出門，因為她是高爾夫球的天后，大家都知道她的大名。後來，我發現我對她的感覺起了變化。我並未愛上她，但對她有一種溫柔之情。她是一個很要強的女子，我記得她還曾經在一場快落敗的比賽中作弊。不過，我沒有向她透露我的情感。我很清楚，我首先要把我和中西部故鄉那位女子的關係處理乾淨。我一向比較坦然，不能繼續欺騙她的感情。

CHAPTER FOUR

P.33

七月下旬，上午九點左右，蓋茨比開車來到我的門口停下，按了按車喇叭。

我打開門時，他說道：「弟兄，早啊！你今天跟我一起吃午餐，我想我們就開車一起去吧。」

我眼睛發亮地盯著他的車子看。

「弟兄，很正吧？你不是有看過嗎？」

「我當然看過了。太炫了！」

蓋茨比的車子，任誰都見過。他的車子是瑰麗的奶油色，有點接近黃色，座椅的皮套是綠色的。車子的內部很寬敞，有各種置物箱，放帽子的、放食物的、放工具的，應有盡有。

我坐上車子，車子一路直驅，穿過西雅歌。

過去一個月以來，我跟他交談過五六次。令我失望的是，他話很少。我不再有那種他是個大人物的印象，只覺得他是隔壁豪宅的主人罷了。所以當他突然轉頭問我說「弟兄，你對我這個人有什麼看法？」時，我感到意外。

我不知如何回答他。

看法

• 你會用多少時間來對一個人產生看法？

• 你曾經改變對某個人的第一印象嗎？為什麼？

• 你的看法會受到別人的影響嗎？

P.34

「我跟你說說我的身世吧，以免你誤信了那些傳聞。」他繼續說道。

看來，他也知道人們在他背後謠傳他一些奇奇怪怪的事。

他說：「我老實跟你說，我是中西部一位有錢人的兒子。我在美國長大，在牛津念書。我的祖先都在牛津念過書，這是我們家族的傳統。」

他說他在牛津上大學時，話很快帶過，而且還斜眼瞄了我一眼，想看我的表情反應。我明白了瓊玥為什麼會不相信他所說的話。他的確有可能幹過罪惡的勾當。

「後來，我的家人都過世了，我繼承了大一筆遺產。」

我看著他，心想他是在捉弄我，然而他的表情很嚴肅。

P.35

「我後來在歐洲各大城市落腳，我住過巴黎、威尼斯和羅馬。我收藏紅寶石、打獵，也畫一些畫，想藉此忘記過去的傷心事。」

我不知道他的話可不可信，但我任他繼續說下去。

「接著，弟兄，就爆發了戰爭。我巴不得可以戰死沙場，但我的命卻好像受到保佑一樣。」

他榮獲過不少勳章。他隨手從口袋裡掏出了一個勳章給我看。

「翻到另一面看看。」他說。

我看著勳章的背面，唸道：「傑‧蓋茨比少校，英勇過人。」

他又給我看了一張他在牛津大學時所拍的照片。

「在我左邊的那一位是道卡斯特伯

111

爵。」他說。

看來他說的都是真的。

「我今天想請你幫我一個大忙，我不想讓你覺得我只是個什麼阿貓阿狗的人。我身邊都是陌生人，那是因為我東飄西蕩，想把發生在我身上的痛苦往事忘掉。」

P.36

他躊躇了一下。

「你今天下午會聽到我的傷心往事。我知道你約了貝克小姐喝茶，她答應了要把事情的始末告訴你。」

我覺得有點生氣，因為我約瓊玥出來，並不是為了要聊傑・蓋茨比。

蓋茨比開快車駛過長島市。就在我們要上橋之前，我聽到旁邊傳來摩托車的噠噠聲。那是警察，他要我們停車。蓋茨比把車子慢下來，從皮夾掏出一張白色的卡片，拿給警察看。

「可以了嗎？弟兄。」

「請原諒，蓋茨比先生，我下次就認得出您了。」

「那是什麼？你在牛津拍的照片？」我問。

「我幫過警長一個忙，他每年都會寄耶誕賀卡給我。」他回答。

我們來到五十二街的一家餐廳，蓋茨比跟我介紹了他一個叫吳善的朋友。

「這家館子是不錯，但我比較喜歡對面的『金都』。我對『金都』有很多的回憶，曾經熟悉的面孔、熟悉的人，就這樣永遠地消失了。他們打死羅西・羅森梭的那個晚上，我始終都記得。當時我們一桌六個人，羅西一整晚大吃大喝。後來，一位服務生說有個人請他到外面去聊聊。他站起身，對我說：『不要讓服務生把我的咖啡收走！』他說完就走出去。他們開了三槍，然後開車逃逸。」

「這件事我記得。」我說。

吳善轉頭看著我。

「我知道你在找做生意的門路。」他說。

P.37

蓋茨比搶話幫我回答說：「不，不是他，他單純是個朋友。那件事我們改天再談。」

「抱歉，我搞錯啦。」他看似有些失望地說。

這時我們點的東西上菜了，吳善先生狼吞虎嚥地吃了起來。

蓋茨比靠過來對我說：「弟兄，抱歉，早上可能讓你生氣了。」

「我不喜歡這樣神祕兮兮的，你為什麼要把貝克小姐扯進來？你不能自己跟我說你的事嗎？」我冷冷淡淡地說。

「她覺得沒關係。」他說。

他看了看手錶，跳了起來，匆匆離開餐廳。

吳善

- 你想吳善的朋友大概都是哪些人？
- 你對一九二〇年代的美國有何認識？

P. 38

「他要去打電話。」吳善一邊目送蓋茨比離開，一邊說道：「他長得真帥，人也很紳士，對吧？」

「是啊。」

「他是牛津出身的。」

「哦！」

「他上過英國的牛津大學。你知道牛津大學嗎？」

「我聽過。」

「全球頂尖的大學。」

「你認識蓋茨比很久了嗎？」我問。

「我認識他好幾年了。大戰剛結束時我就認識他了，我那時和他聊了一個鐘頭，我發現他做人很君子，就是那種你會想把他介紹給媽媽和姊妹認識的人。」

「沒錯。」

「是啊，蓋茨比對女性很守規矩。只要是朋友的妻子，他連看都不看。」

思索一下

- 麻爾·吳善想讓倪克對蓋茨比產生什麼樣的印象？
- 你想蓋茨比和吳善是什麼關係？

蓋茨比回來時，吳善喝完咖啡站了起來，說道：「午餐還不賴，我現在要扔下你們兩位年輕的男士告辭了。」

「麻爾，別急著走。」蓋茨比說，但語氣中並無熱忱。

「你們是翩翩青年，但我是老人家囉。你們繼續坐，聊你們的運動和女人吧。」吳善回答。

P. 39

吳善離開後，蓋茨比說：「他這個人，在紐約無人不知、無人不曉。」

「他是個演員嗎？」

「不是，麻爾·吳善是個賭徒。」蓋茨比有些遲疑地說，接著又冷冷地說：「一九一九年的世界大賽，就是由他賄賂買通的。」

我聽了很吃驚，沒想到單靠他一個人，就愚弄了五千萬人。

「他是怎麼辦到的？」我問。

「他只不過是看中了機會。」

「他怎麼沒被抓去關？」

「弟兄，他們追查不到他。他是個老狐狸。」

詐欺

- 詐欺一個人，和詐欺五千萬人，哪一個罪行比較嚴重？

這頓飯我付了賬。服務生把找的零錢送來時，我看到了湯姆‧卜江南。

「你跟我來一下，我去跟一個人打招呼一下。」我說。

湯姆一看到我，就跳了起來。

「你最近在忙什麼？黛希在氣你都沒有打電話給她。」他說。

「這位是蓋茨比先生，這是卜江南先生。」

他們很快握了握手，我發現蓋茨比露出了尷尬的奇怪表情。

「你怎麼會跑這麼遠來這裡吃飯？」湯姆問。

P. 40

「我和蓋茨比先生一起來吃飯。」

我轉身向蓋茨比先生，他人卻不見了。

（那天下午，瓊玦‧貝克在廣場飯店的茶室裡說道）一九一七年，十月裡的某一天──那時，我正走過黛希的家，那一年她十八歲，是陸宜市最出風頭的女孩。她那時正坐在她的白色小轎車裡，身邊坐了一位穿著制服的軍官。

「哈囉，瓊玦。」黛希對我說。

這位軍官用很特別的神情看著黛希，他的名字叫做傑‧蓋茨比。四年後，我在長島又碰見了這個人，只是我沒認出他來。

我後來開始打高爾夫比賽，就沒有

常去找黛希，不過我聽說了她的事。她那時想去紐約和一位即將出國的軍人道別，不過被她母親給阻攔了。結果第二年，她就嫁給湯姆了。

關係

- 傑‧蓋茨比所說的「傷心往事」是指什麼？
- 你想，傑‧蓋茨比和黛希是什麼關係？
- 你想，黛希的母親為什麼會阻止她去紐約和蓋茨比道別？
- 你覺得父母應該干涉子女的感情嗎？

CHAPTER FIVE

P. 42

我到了凌晨兩點才回到家。我搭的計程車離去之後，我看到蓋茨比朝我走過來。

「弟兄，我們去康尼島走走，坐我的車。」

「太晚了吧。」我回答。

「那麼在我的游泳裡游個泳，我今年夏天都還沒下過游池。」

「我要去睡啦！」

「好吧！」

他看著我，靜待我的反應。

「我和貝克小姐聊過了。我明天會打電話給黛希，請她過來喝個茶。你

哪天方便？」

「您哪天方便？我不想造成你的困擾。」他很快地答道。

「後天如何？」

他想了一會兒，說道：「我要先把草坪整理一下。」

他望著我花園裡的草坪，猶豫了一會兒，又說：「還有一件事……」

「下星期也可以，看你方便。」我說。我想他或許需要多一點時間。

「不，不。」他不知從何說起。接著又說：「你錢賺的不多，是吧，弟兄？」

「是不多。」

「我做了點小生意，或許你會有興趣，可以賺賺錢。這件事就我們兩人個知道，你懂的是吧！」

他的提議明擺了是要回報我幫的這個忙，所以我婉拒了。

P.43

提議

• 倪克為什麼要婉拒？
• 蓋茨比的提議，透露出蓋茨比的什麼事？

隔天早上，我打電話邀請黛希過來喝茶。

「別讓湯姆跟來。」我提醒她說。

我們約好喝茶的那一天下起了雨。十一點時，來了個人修剪我的花園（蓋茨比的花園永遠很整潔）。不久，又有人送來了好多鮮花。

下午三點，蓋茨比慌慌張張走進來，他看起來很緊張。

「午茶都準備好了嗎？」他問。

我帶他進到廚房，給他看我早上買的檸檬蛋糕。

「這樣可以嗎？」

「當然，看起來很好，弟兄。」他說。但我看得出來他有些失望。

P.44

我們走到客廳，他坐了下來。他不時張望窗外的雨景，最後站起來說他要回家。

「沒有人會來喝午茶，太晚了！我不能等一整天。」

「別這麼著急，現在才四點過兩分而已。」

他苦惱地又坐了下來，就在這時，一輛車子往我的房子開了過來。

我走到外面的花園，黛希一看到我，開心地笑了起來。我扶她走出車子。

「你該不會是愛上了我吧？不然為什麼要我單獨一個人過來？」她在我耳邊輕聲說道。

「這是祕密。」

我們走進屋子。我很吃驚的是，房子裡空無一人。這時門外傳來敲門聲。我打開門，是蓋茨比，他人就佇立在雨中。他很快轉身走進客廳。我在門邊等著動靜，在寂靜了一會兒之後，傳來了黛希的笑聲，還有她嘹亮而做作的說話聲：「真高興能再見到你！」

我關上門，走進客廳，和他們待在一起。蓋茨比站在那裡凝視著黛希，黛

115

希坐在椅子的邊緣上，她神色有點惶恐，但舉止還算沉著。

「我們以前認識。」蓋茨比說。

「但有好些年沒有見面了。」黛希很快說道。

「到了十一月，就整整五年了。」蓋茨比脫口而出地說。

P. 45

我坐下來和黛希聊天，一邊喝著茶、吃著檸檬蛋糕。蓋茨比沒有出聲，他用緊張而焦慮的眼神，在我和黛希之間來回張望。我後來留他們獨處了一會兒。

等我再回來時，他們正坐在沙發上凝視著彼此。他們的尷尬時刻看來是過去了。黛希淚流滿面，蓋茨比的變化則令我很意外。他神采煥發，整個房間充滿了他喜悅的光芒。

情緒的變化

• 設想出兩種會讓你「由憂轉喜」和「由喜轉憂」的情況。

「哈囉，弟兄。」蓋茨比說。

「雨停了。」

「是嗎？」他身向黛希說：「雨停了。」

「很高興雨停了，傑。」她的聲音裡帶著喜出望外的喜悅。

「我帶你和黛希去我家走走，我想帶她參觀參觀。」他突然說道。

我們來到花園。黛希指著說：「是那裡嗎？是那棟大房子嗎？」

「你喜歡嗎？」

「我很喜歡，你真的是一個人住在裡頭？」

「我邀請很多有趣的名人過來，所以房子裡頭日日夜夜都會擠滿人。」

P. 46

蓋茨比帶著黛希走過每一間華麗的客廳、音樂廳和書房，黛希嘖嘖稱讚不絕。對蓋茨比來說，這所有東西的價值，似乎都取決於黛希眼裡所做出的反應。他的眼神一刻也沒有離開過黛希。

我們來到他的臥室，站在窗邊，望著海灣。這時又落下了雨絲。

「可惜現在煙雨濛濛的，天氣好的時候，可以看你們對岸的房子。晚上時，你們那邊的碼頭底都會亮起一盞綠燈。」

P. 47

他們望著對岸，黛希這時伸過手挽住蓋茨比的胳臂。這盞綠燈總讓他想起黛希，而此時此刻，黛希就在他身邊，綠燈也不再具有意義了。

在西邊的海上，浮著粉紅色和金色

的雲霞。

「你看那邊！但願我能摘下雲彩，把你放在上面推來推去。」黛希輕聲地說。

我想離開，但他們要我留下。

「我知道接下來要做什麼！我們讓克利本來為我們演奏鋼琴。」蓋茨比說。

我常在泳池邊和海灘上看到克利本。我們坐在音樂廳，他為我們演奏了情歌。

我看看蓋茨比和黛希，他們已經忘記我的存在了。蓋茨比握著黛希的手，黛希則是在蓋茨比的耳邊低訴。蓋茨比轉過臉望著黛希，神情熱切。我站起身，留下他們離開。

CHAPTER SIX

P.48

「傑・蓋茨比」的真實姓名是「詹姆士・葛茲」，他是北達科塔州一位失意農夫的兒子。他在十七歲的時候幫自己改名換姓，在那時候，他在蘇必略湖見識了丹・柯迪先生的遊艇。柯迪當時是一個五十歲的大富翁，靠著銀礦金礦致富。對當時的葛茲來說，這艘遊艇代表了這個世界上的一切榮華富貴。他清楚地看到自己想要成為一個什麼樣的人——他這時也差不多想好了自己的新名字。他在等待時機，準備好好創造一番事業。現在時機來了，他刻意討好柯迪，當遊艇啟程前往西印度群島時，蓋茨比也上了船。

柯迪很快就發現，這個年輕人什麼事情都學得很快，而且很有野心。遊艇上的什麼工作他都做，他後來成了柯迪的祕書。過了五年，在科迪過世之後，「傑・蓋茨比」就不再是當年那個年輕人所創造出來的想像人物。傑・蓋茨比這號人物，已經真實誕生了。

接下來幾個星期，我沒遇到蓋茨比，也沒有他的消息。我大部分的時間都在紐約和瓊玥待在一起。一個星期天的午後，我去了蓋茨比家，沒多久，我們就聽到外面傳來馬蹄聲。那是湯姆・卜江南。看到他，我有些意外。

他是和兩位朋友一起過來的，一個是叫做司龍的男人，另一個是和蓋茨比相識的美女。

「很高興見到你們，歡迎你們光臨寒舍。」蓋茨比站在陽台上說道。

P.49

我確信的是，他們並不在乎蓋茨比是否歡迎他們。他們只是騎馬騎累了，想找個地方歇歇腳，蓋茨比也知道他們來訪的目的，只是湯姆讓他促不安。

他叫來管家，點了飲料，然後說道：「卜江南先生，我想我們以前在哪裡見過面。」

「噢，是啊，這我記得。」湯姆禮貌性地說道。但實際上他不記得了。

「兩個星期以前左右。」

「對啦，你那時和倪克在一起。」

「我也認識令夫人。」

「是嗎？」湯姆轉過臉對著我說：「倪克，你住在這附近？」

「我就住在隔壁。」

「我們得走了，走吧。」司龍對著女士說道。

我跟著湯姆走到陽台。

「我很懷疑他是在哪裡認識黛希的，這年頭的女人家喜歡到處亂跑，什麼奇奇怪怪的男人都遇得上。」

認識新朋友
• 你是如何認識新朋友的？
• 你和新朋友見面時會聊些什麼？

P.50

看來，湯姆有點放心不下黛希，在接下來的星期六晚上，他跟著黛希來到了蓋茨比的派對。在這幾百人的派對上，我們幾個人從頭到尾都在一塊兒。

「你隨便望過去，都可以看到名流人物。」蓋茨比說。

湯姆用傲慢的眼神掃視了一下人群。

「我們平時不太出門，我才想，這裡都沒有我認識的人。」湯姆說。

蓋茨比領著他們向一群又一群的客人作介紹。

「我還沒見過這麼多的名人呢。」黛希興奮地說。

黛希和蓋茨比共舞之後，他們慢步走到我家，在臺階上坐了半個小時。黛希要我待在花園裡把風。

「你待著，以免發生什麼火災或意外之類的事。」她對我說。

P.51

當我們正坐下來吃晚餐時，湯姆又冒了出來。

「我過去跟那幾個人吃飯，可以嗎？有一個傢伙講的事情可有趣了。」湯姆問。

「去吧。如果你想抄下幾個住址，我的金箔小鉛筆在這裡。」黛希說。

一會兒後，她四面張望了一下，看到湯姆和一個女子坐在一塊。

「長得沒有特色，但還算漂亮。」黛希對我說。

聽她這麼一說，我明白到，除了和蓋茨比獨處的那半個鐘頭，黛希玩得並不開心。

他們在等車子開過來時，我陪他們坐在大門前的臺階上等車。

「這個姓蓋茨比的傢伙是什麼來歷？是賣私酒的嗎？」湯姆突然質問道。

「你這是哪裡聽來的？」我問他。

「我不是聽來的，是我自己猜的。像這樣的暴發戶，有很多都是靠賣私酒起家的。」

他接著沉默了半晌。

「要把這些牛頭馬面都找來這個派對上，很費事的。」

「這些人比我們認識的那些人有趣多了。」黛希說。

「可是你看起來不是很有興致。」

「我有啊。」她回答。

「我想知道蓋茨比是何方神聖，是在搞什麼事業的，我一定要打聽清楚。」湯姆說。

「我現在就可以告訴你，他是在開連鎖藥局的。」她說。

他們的車子這時駛上了車道。

「倪克，晚安。」黛希說。

P.52

那夜我待到很晚，蓋茨比要我等他。最後他來到花園，他看起來有點疲憊，

不過眼睛炯炯有神。

「黛希不喜歡這個派對。」他開口就說。

「她當然喜歡啦。」

他沒有作聲，我猜他是有心事。

「我覺得我離她好遠，無法讓她了解。」他說。

「了解什麼事？」

他要黛希跟湯姆攤牌說「我從來就沒有愛過你」，用這樣一句話就可以把這四年來的關係一筆勾銷，換回自由。這樣，他們就可以一起回到陸宜市去結婚，就像回到五年前他所計畫的那樣。

「但她就是聽不懂我所說的，她以前能懂，現在就不懂了。」他說。

他停住不說話，開始來回踱步。

「你不要對她要求太多，過去的事無法重演。」我勸他說。

「為什麼不？我要讓每件事都回到過去。」他大喊道。

這一晚，他細數了陳年往事。他提到他和黛希的初吻，那發生在五年前的一個秋夜裡。他覺得沒有什麼東西是他得不到的，他已經可以看到自己的未來，然而就在那之後，他的生活開始變得一團亂。他失去了某種東西，大概是失去了對自己的想法吧。如果他能回到過去，慢慢地再重新走

過一遍，或許就能找回如今所失去的東西。

CHAPTER SEVEN

P.54

一個週末夜晚，蓋茨比宅院的燈火未亮。來訪的一輛輛汽車，稍停片刻之後，又一輛輛地開走。我想他是不是病了，就走去他家探問。來開門的是一個我不認識的管家。

「蓋茨比先生是身體欠安嗎？」

「不是！」管家粗聲粗氣地說。

「我不太放心，請跟他說賈若維先生來過。」

「賈若維，好吧，我會轉告。」

之後，我的管家跟我說，蓋茨比把所有的僕人都換掉，另外雇了六個人。管家說，她覺得那六個人壓根不是什麼僕人。

隔天，蓋茨比打電話給我。

「你是準備離開嗎？我聽說你把僕人都換掉了。」我問。

「我不想聽到別人閒言閒語，黛希下午常會過來。」

他因為黛希有微詞，所以把僕人都換掉了。

「黛希問你，明天要不要一起去她家吃午飯？貝克小姐也會去。」

沒多久，換黛希打電話來，說她很高興我要去。我覺得她和蓋茨比之間一定發生了什麼事。

蓋茨比和黛希

• 蓋茨比和黛希之間，有可能是出了什麼事？

P.55

第二天，天氣很熱。我和蓋茨比來到卜江南公館，一個女僕領我們來到一間蔭暗的客廳。黛希和瓊玥正躺在大沙發上，一旁的電扇呼呼吹著。湯姆沒有在客廳裡。

「我們好懶得動。」她們說。

蓋茨比站在紅色地毯的中央，他打量四周，看得出神。

這時，湯姆走進來，伸出了手。

「蓋茨比先生！很高興見到您……倪克……」

「給我們拿冷飲來吧！」黛希喊道。

等湯姆一走出客廳，黛希立刻站起來，走到蓋茨比面前，在他的唇上親吻了一下。

「你知道我愛你。」她喃喃地說。

P.56

湯姆這時端著冷飲走進來。

湯姆遞了一杯給蓋茨比。蓋茨比說：

「看起來很冰涼！」

我們一邊喝著冷飲，一邊聊著天氣。接著湯姆對蓋茨比說：「我們去外面，我帶你到處看看。」

他們走到外面的遊廊上，我跟在後面。

我們望著海灣，蓋茨比指著對岸說：「我的房子就在那邊，剛好跟你們的房子對望。」

「可不是嘛。」湯姆回答。

我們在那裡待了一會兒後，走回蔭暗的客廳用餐。

後來，黛希說：「我們下午要做什麼好呢？天氣熱得讓人頭暈眼花。我們進城吧！」

蓋茨比轉身盯著她看。

「哈，你看起來真酷！」黛希說。

他們四目交接，旁若無人。

她的眼神對他流露出無限愛意。湯姆也看出來了，他很吃驚。他看看蓋茨比，又看看黛希。

P.57

肢體語言

• 黛希不用言語透露愛意，而是用眼睛傳達，這就是所謂的「肢體語言」。

• 你能從別人的肢體語言，讀出喜怒哀樂嗎？

「走吧，我們進城去。」湯姆說。

湯姆站起身子，但其他人都坐在原位不動。

「什麼？現在？要穿這樣子去？」黛希問。

120

湯姆沒有回答。

「好吧,不過我們要花一點時間準備一下。」

她和瓊玥走上樓,我們三位男士在屋外站著。

「我們要帶點喝的上路嗎?」黛希從樓上的窗口往樓下喊道。

「我帶瓶威士忌好了。」湯姆說罷,便走進屋子。

P.58

不久,當他走出來時,後面跟著黛希和瓊玥。

「坐我的車吧。」蓋茨比說。

「不,你開我的跑車,我開你的車子。」

蓋茨比並不喜歡這種安排。

「黛希,來吧,我用這輛車載你。」湯姆一邊說道,一邊拉著黛希走向蓋茨比的車子。

湯姆打開車門,黛希卻轉身走掉。

「你載倪克和瓊玥,我們開跑車在後面跟著。」她一邊說,一邊走向蓋茨比。

我和瓊玥、湯姆進了蓋茨比的車子。湯姆發動車子離開。

「你們看到了嗎?」湯姆說。

「看到什麼?」

「你們當我是二楞子嗎?也許我是二楞子沒錯,但我已經在調查蓋茨比的底細了!」

「你有查出來他是讀牛津大學的嗎?」瓊玥說。

「讀牛津大學!」湯姆不屑地重複道。

「你要是瞧不起他這個人,幹嘛還找他來?」瓊玥問。

「是黛希要找他來的。在我們結婚之前,他們兩個就認識了。」

「我們的汽油夠嗎?」我問。

「還夠開到城裡。」湯姆說。

「那邊有個修車行,我可不想在這個大熱天裡被卡在車子裡頭。」瓊玥說。

湯姆
- 湯姆心裡頭是什麼樣的滋味?
- 他為什麼會想開蓋茨比的車子?
- 湯姆有懷疑黛希和蓋茨比以前是情侶嗎?

P.59

湯姆不耐煩地把車開到「魏爾森」的看板下停下來。過了一會兒,老闆走了出來。

「給我們加點汽油!」湯姆喊道。

「我病啦。」魏爾森站著不動地說道。

「你怎麼啦?」

121

「我身體垮了，很需要錢。你那輛舊車子呢？」

「這輛你喜歡嗎？我上星期才買的。」湯姆說。

「這輛車子的顏色很漂亮，但太貴啦。」

「你要錢是要幹嘛？」

「我在這個地方打滾很久了，我想和妻子搬去西部。」

「你老婆想搬去西部？」湯姆喊道。這讓他很意外。

「她跟我提了好多年了，現在不管如何，她就是要搬去西部。」

這時跑車從我們身邊呼嘯而過，蓋茨比和黛希跟我們招了招手。

「我最近覺得事情有點蹊蹺，所以想離開，想要那輛車子。」魏爾森說。

「多少錢？」

「一塊兩角。」

我發現，魏爾森沒有對湯姆起過疑心。魏爾森發現茉桃背著他搞鬼，所以悶出了病。我看著湯姆，湯姆在不到一個小時以前，也嚐到了同樣的滋味。

「明天我就把車子開過來給你。」湯姆說。

P.60

這時，茉桃・魏爾森從修車行樓上的窗口往樓下俯視。她不是在看湯姆，而是盯著瓊玥瞧。她的眼裡燃燒著妒火，因為她以為瓊玥就是湯姆的妻子。

湯姆的心裡現在備受煎熬。一個小時以前，他還安安穩穩地坐享齊人之福，誰知道現在卻好像兩頭都落空。他猛踩油門，很快追上他的藍色跑車。黛希這

時跟我們招手，要我們停下來。

「我們要去哪裡啊？」黛希喊道。

「我們去電影！」瓊玥說。

「電影院裡頭太熱了，你們去就好。我們去兜兜風，待會再跟你們碰面。」黛希回答。

「不要在街上吵這個，跟我到廣場飯店去。」湯姆火大地說。

我們在飯店裡租了間大客廳，裡頭很熱，沒有空調。

「再開扇窗戶吧。」黛希命令道。

「別管天氣熱不熱了，你這樣嘮嘮叨叨只會更熱。」湯姆煩噪說。

他拿出威士忌，把酒擱在桌子上。

「何必找她的碴呢，弟兄？是你自己要進城來的。」蓋茨比說。

「這是你得意的口頭禪，是嗎？」湯姆尖銳地說。

「你是指什麼？」

「我指『弟兄』，你這是哪裡學來的？」

「湯姆，如果你要做人身攻擊，我就走！我們點些冰塊來做薄荷酒啦。」黛希說。

P. 62

湯姆點了冰塊，我們閒聊了一會兒。這時湯姆說：「蓋茨比先生，我聽說你上過牛津大學。」

「我是在那裡念過書。」

「什麼時候的事？」

「一九一九年的時候，我在牛津待了五個月，所以也不算是真正的牛津人。」

這時服務生送來了薄荷和冰塊。

「大戰結束後，他們提供名額給一些軍官，可以去英國或法國念大學。軍官可以自由選擇。」

我對蓋茨比又有了不同的認識。這不是第一次了。

「湯姆，打開威士忌，我來給你做杯薄荷酒，喝了就不會覺得自己很蠢了。」

生氣

• 你是個容易生氣的人嗎？
• 你會因為什麼樣的事情而生氣？
• 你生氣時會怎樣？

「等等，我還有個問題要問蓋茨比先生。」湯姆尖銳地說。

「你問吧！」蓋茨比禮貌地回答。

「你到底想在我家裡製造什麼樣的糾紛？」

事情這時終於攤開了，這是蓋茨比所樂於見到的。

「他沒有要製造糾紛，在製造糾紛的是你！拜託，你也稍微控制一下你自己。」黛希說。

「什麼！控制我自己？難道我應該乖乖坐在這裡，讓這個來路不明的阿貓阿狗把我的老婆給拐走？」湯姆喊道。

「我也有話要對你說，弟兄。」蓋茨比開始說道。

「不要！」黛希打斷他的話，她猜得出蓋茨比的意圖。「我們走吧。我們都各自回家吧！」

P. 63

「也好，湯姆，走吧，沒人想喝酒了。」我站起身子，說道。

「我想聽聽蓋茨比先生要跟我講什麼！」湯姆說。

「你的妻子並不愛你，她從來就沒愛過你。她愛的是我！」蓋茨比說。

「你這個瘋子！」湯姆叫道。

蓋茨比站起來，臉上露出亢奮的神情。

「她會嫁給你，是因為我以前是個窮光蛋，而且她也不想再等我了。你們的婚姻從頭到尾都是一場錯誤，她的心裡只有我，沒有其他人！」

瓊玥和我想開溜，但湯姆和蓋茨比要我們兩個留下。

「你在胡說什麼？給我說清楚！」湯姆說。

「我說過的，我和黛希相愛已經有五年了！」蓋茨比回答。

「你們多久見一次面？」湯姆轉向黛希問道。

「弟兄，我們很久沒見面了，但我們心裡頭一直都深愛著彼此，這件事你並不知道。我有時一想到這裡，就忍不住想笑。」

「就這樣？」湯姆問道，接著他破口大罵說：「你這個瘋子！五年前的事情

是怎樣，我沒話說，因為那時候我還不認識黛希，但其他的事都是你亂說的！黛希是因為愛我，才嫁給我！她現在還是一樣愛我！」

「不對！」蓋茨比搖搖頭說。

「對！雖然她有時候會一些奇怪的想法，或是搞不清楚狀況，但是我愛她！我有時候會出去荒唐一下，把自己弄得一身腥，但我都還是會回到她身邊。我心裡頭一直是愛著她的！」

P.64

「你真叫人噁心！」黛希轉身向著我，說道：「你知道我們為什麼離開芝加哥嗎？我很意外你竟然沒有聽過他在那裡所做的醜事！」

「黛希，那都不要緊了。你就跟他說真話，說你從來就沒有愛過他。」蓋茨比說。

她用求助的眼神看著我和瓊玥。事情已經走到了這般田地，她現在才搞清楚狀況。

黛希
- 黛希知道自己愛的是誰嗎？
- 為什麼她愛的可能是蓋茨比，也可能是湯姆？
- 你想她會選擇誰？

「我從來就沒有愛過他。」我們聽得出來黛希的語氣中帶著勉強。

「我們在佳萍蘭（譯註：一座位於檀香山的大公園）的時候，你也沒愛過我嗎？」湯姆質問道。

「沒有。」

「那麼，那一天，我把你從「甜酒缽」（譯註：一座死火山）上抱下來，以免弄濕了你的鞋子，那時候你也不愛我嗎？」湯姆的言語中帶著柔情。

「別說了！」黛希說罷，轉身看著蓋茨比，哭了起來，「你要的太多了，我現在很愛你，這還不夠嗎？過去的事我無法挽回。我曾經愛過他，但我也愛過你。」

「你『也』愛過我？」蓋茨比說。

「她是騙你的！黛希和我之間有很多不為人知的點點滴滴，這些事情我們一輩子也不會忘記！」湯姆說。

蓋茨比顯得很震驚，他說：「我想和黛希單獨談談，她現在太激動了。」

P.65

「就算我們單獨談，我也不能說我沒有愛過湯姆，那不是真話。」黛希說。

「當然不是真話！從今以後，我要更加珍惜你。」湯姆附和道。

「你還聽不懂嗎？黛希要離開你！」蓋茨比說。

「你亂說！」

「我的確是要離開你。」她費勁地說出

口。

「她不會離開我的！她才不會跟一個騙子走！」湯姆口氣堅定地說。

「我不要跟騙子走！我們走吧。」黛希喊道。

P.66

湯姆把身子挨向蓋茨比，說道：「我知道你和麻爾·吳善有來往，我查了你的底細，明天還會有真相。」

「弟兄，悉聽尊便。」

「我也知道你的藥局在搞什麼名堂。」湯姆接著轉身向我和瓊玥說：「我打聽出來了，他們在這裡、在芝加哥買了很多藥局，然後在藥局裡偷賣私酒。這只是他所的做其中一個買賣而已，他還準備幹更大的勾當。我一看到他這個人，就知道他是個賣私酒的人。他被我說中了！」

我看著黛希，她嚇得目瞪口呆。她看看蓋茨比，又看看丈夫。我又看了一下瓊玥，她露出不感興趣的神情，她的這種表情我很熟。接著，我再看看蓋茨比，他那種自信沉著的態度已不復見。

自信

- 自信的人通常會表現出什麼樣的行為舉止？
- 沒有自信的人，又會表現出什麼樣的行為舉止？
- 什麼樣的經驗，可以幫助人們建立自信？

蓋茨比激動地向黛希做解釋，他矢口否認一切，為自己辯白，但黛希已經聽

不進去了。「湯姆，求求你！我再也受不了。」

P.67

她神色驚慌，不管她有過什麼想法和勇氣，如今都已經煙消雲散。

「回家吧，黛希，蓋茨比先生會開他的車子送你回去。他不會對你怎樣的，他知道這段愚蠢的風流韻事已經結束了。」湯姆說。

蓋茨比和黛希半句話也沒有說地離開。等到我們跟湯姆坐上跑車，動身回長島時，已經七點鐘了。湯姆一路上沒停過地又說又笑，但感覺上卻離我和瓊玥很遠。我們過了橋之後，瓊玥把她白皙的臉靠在我的肩膀上，握住我的手。這一天，剛好是我的生日。我已經到了而立之年。

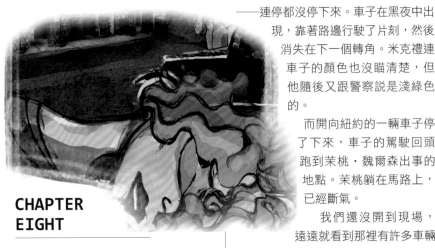

CHAPTER EIGHT

P.69

下午五點，在魏爾森修車行旁邊開咖啡廳的希臘年輕人米克禮，他走過來修車行，想找人聊天。他看到魏爾森待在辦公間裡，病情看起來很嚴重。他勸魏爾森上床休息，但魏爾森說他不想錯過生意。這時，樓上忽然大吵大鬧起來。

「我把我老婆鎖在房間裡，等我們要搬家了，我再放她出來。」

米克禮很訝異魏爾森會說出這種話。他想知道發生了什麼事，但是魏爾森一個字也不肯說。這時，來了幾個工人走進他的咖啡廳，他就先告辭了。一直到七點過後，米克禮才又走出來外面。他聽到修車行樓下傳來魏爾森太太大吼大叫的聲音。她正在對著老公咆哮。

過了沒多久，魏爾森太太跑出門來。這時，米克禮還來不及做出反應，事情就已經發生了。

那輛「凶車」──這是報紙上的說法──連停都沒停下來。車子在黑夜中出現，靠著路邊行駛了片刻，然後消失在下一個轉角。米克禮連車子的顏色也沒瞄清楚，但他隨後又跟警察說是淺綠色的。

而開向紐約的一輛車子停了下來，車子的駕駛回頭跑到茉桃·魏爾森出事的地點。茉桃躺在馬路上，已經斷氣。

我們還沒開到現場，遠遠就看到那裡有許多車輛和人群。

「有人撞車了！這樣也好，魏爾森就有生意可以做了。」湯姆說。

湯姆把車子停在修車行前面。

「我們去看看。」湯姆說。

P.70

這時修車行裡頭傳出號啕大哭的聲音，那是魏爾森的聲音。「天啊！天啊！」他不斷地哭喊著。

「這裡出事了。」湯姆一邊說，一邊抬頭想望過人群。

這時，他突然發出了一個奇怪的聲音，開始擠開人群走到前面。我和瓊玥跟在後頭。茉桃的屍體裹在一條毯子裡，橫陳在牆邊的一張桌子上。湯姆俯身看看她，然後轉向一名正在小本子上抄寫姓名的警員。

「她發生什麼事了？」

「被車子撞到，當場死亡。」

「當場死亡？」湯姆重複道。

馬路上的意外

• 馬路上發生意外,通常會有哪些原因?

• 人們可以怎麼做,以便減少意外事故?

「她衝進馬路,當時路上有兩輛車子,她是被從紐約那邊開來的車子給撞上的。」米克禮說。

「肇事的車子是一輛很大的黃色新車。」另一個人說。

「你親眼看到的?」員警問。

「不是,是後來有一輛很大的黃色新車很快地從我旁邊開過。」

這些話傳到了魏爾森的耳裡。

「你們不用跟我說是什麼車子!這我很清楚!」魏爾森喊道。

湯姆的肩膀肌肉緊繃了起來。他朝魏爾森走過去,抓住他的手臂。

P.71

「你冷靜一下。我剛剛才從紐約開到這裡,我開我的跑車過來給你,我下午開的那輛黃色車子,並不是我的。」湯姆說。

員警打量著湯姆。

「你說什麼?」員警質問。

「我是魏爾森的朋友,魏爾森說他看過那輛肇事的車子,那是一輛黃色的車子。」湯姆說。

「你的車子是什麼顏色的?」員警起了疑心地問道。

「我的是藍色的跑車。」

「我們才剛從紐約那邊開過來。」我

說。

車子一直開在我們後面的駕駛,幫我們證實了這一點。員警於是轉身掉頭走開。

湯姆扶著魏爾森走回辦公間,讓他坐在椅子上,然後自己再走回來。

「有人要陪魏爾森坐一下嗎?」湯姆問。

有兩個人走進門去,湯姆隨手把門帶上。

「我們走吧。」湯姆小聲對我說。

一開始,湯姆慢慢地把車駛離,後來他把油門踩到底,跑車在黑夜裡飛馳而去。我聽到嗚咽的聲音,看到湯姆的臉上滑下了眼淚。

「那個孬種!他的車子連停都沒停。」他情緒激動,用顫抖的聲音說道。

我們來到他家,湯姆抬頭看了一下二樓,燈光是亮的。

「黛希到家了。倪克,我忘了要先送你回西雅歌。」湯姆說。

P.72

湯姆這時冷靜了下來,心情平復了些。

「我們今天晚上也不能做什麼,我叫輛計程車送你回家吧。」

他推開大門。

「進來吧。你可以坐在廚房等,順便吃個東西,如果餓的話。」

「不用了,謝謝。我在外面等就好。」

瓊玥用手挽著我的胳臂。

「倪克,你不想進來?」

「不啦,謝謝。」

我覺得不是很舒服,想自己一個人靜

「死了。」

「我想也是。我跟黛希說應該是死了,她表現得滿鎮定的。」

他說話的樣子,顯得黛希的反應比茉桃的命還重要。

「我從一條小路開車回西雅歌,把車子停進車庫。我想沒有人看到我們,但我不是很確定。」他繼續說道。

他這時候已經讓我覺得很反感,所以我連數落他都沒有。

P.74

「那個女人是誰?」蓋茨比問。

「她姓魏爾森,她丈夫是修車行的老闆。這件事情到底是怎麼發生的?」

「我想把駕駛盤扳過來……」他話說到一半打住,我頓時猜到了真相。

「開車的是黛希?」

半晌之後,他才答道:「是,不過我當然要說是我開的。我們離開紐約的時候,她心很煩,說她想開車,讓自己冷靜一下。後來,那個女人衝出馬路,當時我們對面有一輛車子迎面開來,和我們交錯而過。這是前後不到一分鐘所發生的事。我覺得那個女人好像以為我們是她認識的人,還向我們招手。我猜她應該會當場就被撞死。」

他停了一會兒。

「天一亮,黛希就會沒事了,我要在這裡守候她。她把自己關在房間裡。只要湯姆有什麼野蠻的舉動,她就會閃燈給我看。」

一靜,但瓊玥還流連了一下。

「現在才九點半。」她說。

但我今天跟他們待在一起也夠久了,包括瓊玥。瓊玥看著我的臉,讀出了我的心思。她轉過身,走進屋子。

瓊玥·貝克

• 瓊玥·貝克是怎樣的一個人?
• 你想倪克會繼續和瓊玥約會嗎?
• 瓊玥這個角色在故事裡的重要性如何?

在管家打電話叫計程車時,我兩手抱著頭坐在臺階上。

隨後,我沿著車道慢慢從房子面前走開,準備到大門口去等車。

突然,蓋茨比從灌木叢裡出來,走到小路上。

「你在幹什麼?」我問。

P.73

「我就在這裡待著,弟兄。你在路上有看到出了什麼事嗎?」他說。

「有!」

「她死了嗎?」

蓋茨比

- 蓋茨比對車禍的反應是怎樣的？
- 這透露出了他的什麼性格？

「他不會對她怎樣的，他現在想的不是她。」我說。

「我不信任他，弟兄。」

這時我閃過一個想法。湯姆要是發現開車的是黛希，他心裡就會明白一些事情。

「你在這裡等著，我去看看他們有沒有吵鬧的跡象。」我說。

P.75

我轉身走回去，往廚房的窗戶望進去，看到黛希和湯姆彼此面對面地坐在桌前。黛希不時抬眼看著湯姆，然後點點頭地表示同意。我眼前這兩個人看起來很親密，他們沒有什麼特別的情緒，好像在談著什麼計畫似的。

我走回蓋茨比身邊，他問道：「都沒事吧？」

「沒事。你也回去休息吧。」

他搖了搖頭。

「我要在這裡等黛希上床睡覺。晚安，弟兄。」

我轉身離開，留他在月光下守著。

CHAPTER NINE

P.76

我整夜都無法入睡。未天亮時，我聽見一輛計程車開上蓋茨比的車道。我跳下床，穿上衣服，往他家走去。

他的大門是開著的，他人在大廳裡，看起來很疲憊。

「沒什麼事，我在那裡等著，四點鐘左右，她走到窗口，站了一會兒，然後把燈關掉。」

我們走進客廳，打開窗戶，在黑暗中抽著菸。

「你要趕快離開，他們會追查你的車子。」我說。

「弟兄，你是說『現在』就離開？」

他還不想離開，他要先知道黛希的打算才肯走。這是他最後的一絲希望。

這個夜裡，他跟我說了丹‧柯迪的事，但他真正想聊的是黛希。他說，她是他所認識的第一個「大家閨秀」。她帶他去她家，他很訝異她家是那麼漂亮。她家中的每一樣東西都刺激著他的想像，他覺得這個房子裡一定充滿了情史和祕密，而他自己卻沒有資格進到這個房子裡。因為他是個窮小子，沒有任何的背景，有的只是對未來的夢想和野心。不過，他讓黛希以為他出身良好。

他打算跟她玩玩，然後一走了之。他並不打算對她付出感情。

大戰結束後，他想回到家鄉，卻陰錯陽差地被送到了牛津。黛希在來信上表達自己有多麼的絕望。她不明白他為什麼不能回來？她需要他在身邊。

P.77

她需要知道自己的選擇是正確的。

黛希開始感受到外界的壓力——在她所處的人世間裡，充滿著鮮花和樂隊、勢利和虛偽。她想立刻就解決自己的終身大事，而就在那年春天，她認識了湯姆・卜江南。

未來

• 你有計畫過你的未來嗎？
• 你以後想做什麼事嗎？
• 你想去什麼地方嗎？

「我不覺得她愛過湯姆。湯姆昨天跟她講那些話，把她嚇唬住了，他把我說成是一個一文不值的騙子。她不知道她自己在說什麼。她當初在嫁給他時，可能有愛過他一陣子，但她更愛的是我。你懂嗎？」

這時候已經九點，我得去上班。

「我中午再打電話給你。」我說。

「不，弟兄，我猜黛希也會打給我。」

「我猜也是。」

「那麼，再見吧。」

我們握了握手。走到大門口時，我轉過身，大聲對他說：「他們都是混蛋，把他們全部的人加起來，還比不上你一個人。」

P.78

我很高興自己說了這些話，這是我唯一對他說過的好話，因為我從頭到尾都沒有認同過他。

我努力想做點工作，卻在坐位上打了瞌睡。快到中午時，電話聲叫醒了我。是瓊玥打來的。

「我已經離開黛希家了，正準備要去南安敦。你昨天晚上不是很貼心，但我還是想見你。」

「我也想見你。」

「那我就不去南安敦了，下午來城裡找我吧！」

「今天下午不行。」

我們聊了一會兒，最後有人掛了電話。我不記得是誰掛的，我只記得我當天一整天都不想再跟她講話。

我打電話到蓋茨比家。我打了四次，電話都在佔線中。

P.79

現在我要回溯一下，說說我們前晚離開修車行後，那裡接下來所發生的事情。

意外發生之後，米克禮陪著魏爾森。魏爾森很混亂，一直到了凌晨三點，他才開始談起那輛黃色的車子。他說，他有方法可以查出車主。他又提到，兩個

月以前，她老婆有一次鼻青臉腫地回到家。

「是他殺了她。」魏爾森説。

「是誰殺了她？」

「我有法子可以查出來。」

「喬治，這是意外事件。」

「是車子裡的男人撞死了她。她跑出去要跟他講話，可是車子沒有停下來。」

魏爾森

• 魏爾森要如何查出來車子的車主？

• 他如果查出來了，會做什麼事？

米克禮待到早上六點才離開魏爾森。十點時，他又來到修車行，但是沒有看到魏爾森。警方猜想他當天早上去追了黃色車子的車主。下午兩點半，魏爾森來到了西雅歌，跟別人問了去蓋茨比家的路。

P. 80

下午兩點，蓋茨比換上泳裝。他跟管家説，如果有人打電話來，就去叫他接電話。在去游泳池之前，他先走到車庫，拿了橡皮墊子。

這期間都沒有人打電話來。

司機聽到了槍聲，但他沒有去做檢查。他後來説，他當時覺得這不是什麼大不了的事。

當天傍晚，我從車站開車直驅蓋茨比家。我想屋子裡的每一個人都知道發生了什麼事情，但大家都默不作聲。在一片鴉雀無聲中，司機、男管家、園丁和我匆匆來到游泳池邊。風在水面上吹起微微的漣漪，把橡皮墊子和躺在上面的人，緩緩地往池邊推去。

在我們將蓋茨比的屍體抬回屋子裡的途中，我們看見魏爾森的屍體，他躺在離池邊不遠的草坪上。

思索一下

• 蓋茨比的死在意料之中嗎？

• 又是誰殺了魏爾森的？

CHAPTER TEN

P. 82

那一晚和第二天，員警、攝影師和新聞記者，他們一批批地來了又去，去了又來。

米克禮在接受盤問時，提到了魏爾森懷疑妻子與別人有染。但茉桃的妹妹凱薩琳説，她發誓茉桃從來沒有見過蓋茨比這個人，而且他們夫妻的感情很好。魏爾森被判定為「悲傷過度，一時失去理智」，然後案子就結案了。

從我打電話到西雅歌鎮上報案之後，每一件事情都

會打聽到我這邊來，後來所有處理上的事情就變成我在負責，因為除了我，沒有其他人感興趣。

我在屍體被發現後的半個鐘頭，撥了電話給黛希，但是黛希已經和湯姆出門了。

隔天早上，我稍了信給吳善，要他搭最近的一班地鐵過來。他回信給我，說他太忙了，抽不了身，而且他也不想跟這件事有任何牽連。我開始對蓋茨比起了更多的憐憫之情。

到了第三天，從明尼蘇達州來了一封電報，上面署名「亨利·C·葛茲」，對方說會立刻趕來，要求等他到達後再舉行葬禮。

那是蓋茨比年邁的父親，他的臉色很悲傷，在這樣的九月天就裹上了一件長外套。他看起來身心交瘁，我就帶他到音樂廳，並且要管家幫他送一杯牛奶過來。

「我在芝加哥的報紙上看到了新聞。」他說。

「我不知道怎麼聯絡上您。」

「吉米現在在哪裡？」

我指著客廳。

P. 83

他慢慢站起來，走到兒子躺著的房間裡。過一會兒後，他老淚縱橫地走出來。

「他這一生還大有可為的，他還年輕，頭腦又這麼好。」

「您說的沒錯。」我局促不安地說。

倪克

• 如果你是倪克，你現在心裡頭想的是什麼？

• 為什麼現在會「對蓋茨比生起了更多的憐憫之情」？

• 如果是你，你會繼續待在西雅歌嗎？

在葬禮當天的那個上午，我去找了吳善。

「你是他最親近的朋友，所以我想你會想來送他最後一程。」我說。

「我是想，但我不能去。有人被殺，我都會撇得遠遠的。我一向保持冷漠，不過現在……」

我回到西雅歌，走到隔壁去探望葛茲先生。

「你們最近有見過面嗎？」我問。

「他兩年前有回來看過我，幫我買了我現在住的房子。他離家出走時，我們很傷心，但我明白他那樣做是有道理的。他知道他會有一番作為。他發跡之後，對我很大方。」

時間將近三點，路德教會的牧師已經來到。我們又等了半個鐘頭，但是沒有看到任何人前來。

P. 85

　　我們前往墓地時，天空飄著雨。我和葛茲先生、牧師坐在大轎車裡，有四、五個傭人和西雅歌鎮的郵差，他們搭蓋茲比的旅車接著到來。後來又來了一輛車子，我在蓋茲比的書房見過那個人。

　　我試著回想蓋茲比，但他已經變得模糊。我心裡只想著，黛希連來一封信或一束花都沒有。

　　葬禮結束後，我們快步穿過雨中，回到車上。

　　「我沒能趕上在他的房子前集合。」他說。

　　「沒有人趕上。」

　　「他們以前一來就是好幾百個人！真可憐！」他說。

　　蓋茲比過世之後，東部對我的意義已經變得不一樣。我決定離開。

　　我在離開之前和瓊玥·貝克碰了面。我們聊了聊我們兩個人之間的事，又談到我後來遇到的一些事情。等我講完之後，她告訴我，她和別人訂婚了。我不太相信，但我還是做出了驚訝的反應。我突然覺得自己在自討沒趣，我站起身子，跟她道別。我很懊惱，有部分原因是因為我對她還有感情，我心裡很難過。

P. 86

　　十月的一個午後，我碰到了湯姆，他那時正走在第五大道上。他看到我，伸出了手，但我沒有回應他。

　　「倪克，怎麼啦？你不想跟我握手？」

　　「沒錯，你知道我是怎麼看你這個人的。」

　　「你瘋啦，倪克。」他很快地回道。

　　「你那天下午對魏爾森說了什麼？」我問。我懷疑魏爾森先去找過湯姆，然後才找上蓋茲比。

　　他不發一語地看著我，我知道他想講什麼。

　　我掉頭想走，他抓住了我的手臂。

　　「我跟他說了實話。他來到我家門口，想要闖到樓上來，他那時候已經瘋了。他手裡握著槍，跟我問車子的主人是誰。他準備殺掉我，我只好招了，蓋茲比也是罪有應得的。他唬弄你，就像他唬弄黛希一樣。他心腸好狠，他撞了茉桃，車子連停一下也沒有。」

　　我無話可說，除了這個說不出來的事實。我無法寬恕或接受他，然而他所做的有他的道理。我和他握了手。如果我不和他握手，會顯得我很幼稚，因為我突然覺得我不過是在跟一個還沒長大的小孩說話。

　　在我離開西雅歌的最後一個晚上，我去蓋茲比空蕩蕩的房子回顧了一下。我走到他的海灘上，現在是冬天，大部分的海濱大別墅都封了起來。我懷念著蓋茲比，我記得他伸出手臂，指向黛希那邊的碼頭底的綠燈。當時他的夢想似乎就在眼前，他不可能抓不住。然而他有所不知，他的那個夢想，早已棄他而去。

ANSWER KEY

Before Reading

Page 8

❶ (possible answers) party, garden, steps, house, lights, fence, seats, chairs, table, glasses, drinks, elegant, fun, conversation, dancing, toast

Page 10

❼ a) 3   b) 5   c) 4   d) 1   e) 6   f) 2

Page 11

❽ (possible answers)
1. Places to live--apartment, mansion, palace
2. Things outside a house--drive, gate, lawn, path
3. External parts of a house--front door, porch, steps, terrace, verandah, garage
4. Internal parts of a house--hall, kitchen, music room, upstairs
5. Places--jail, restaurant, station

❾ a) verandah   b) drive   c) lawn   d) gate

❿ a) lawn   b) verandah   c) drive   d) gate

Page 18

Tom remarks that he hasn't heard of the bank where Nick works. And he advises Nick not to believe what Daisy tells him.

Page 23

(possible answer) So she won't expect him to leave her.

Page 29

(possible answer) Nobody really knows what he did because Gatsby may not want people to know the truth.

Page 36

(possible answer) His friends were most likely bootleggers and smugglers of alcohol. In the 1920s there was prohibition in America and it was illegal to sell alcohol.

Page 38

He is trying to tell Nick that he can trust Gatsby. The men are business partners of some kind.

Page 41

(possible answers) The sad thing was when Daisy got married. Jay Gatsby and Daisy were lovers, they are about to become lovers again. Daisy's mother didn't want her to become involved with someone from a lower social class.

Page 43

Nick doesn't want to be 'bought' or bribed by Gatsby. It tells us that Gatsby thinks that he can use money to get what he wants.

Page 58

(possible answer) Tom feels hurt and angry. He wants to drive Gatsby's car as he wants George and Myrtle Wilson to see it. He probably suspects that Daisy and Gatsby had a relationship before Daisy married him.

Page 64

(possible answer) Daisy seems to be confused; she doesn't really know who she loves. She might love Gatsby because of the relationship they have and the closeness they once had. She might love Tom because they are married and have a child.

Page 72

We know she is a professional golfer, and that she is ambitious and quite well-known. Jordan is a minor character, but she is important to the story. As a friend of Daisy's she is able to give important information to Nick and bring the plot

forward. She also represents a new type of woman: modern, ambitious, aggressive and dishonest.

Page 74

Gatsby is more concerned about Daisy's reaction what really happened. This shows he is very self-centered and unaware of reality.

Page 79

He saw Tom driving the car, so he will ask him.

Page 81

No, Gatsby wasn't expecting to be killed. Wilson killed himself.

After Reading

Page 90

7 a) F b) T c) F d) F e) F f) T
g) F h) F
8 a) neighbor b) second cousin
c) business partner d) sister
e) husband f) father

Page 91

9 a) 1, b) 7, c) 4, d) 3, e) 6, f) 8, g) 2, h) 5

Page 92

11 a) Daisy b) Jordan Baker
c) Tom Buchanan d) Myrtle Wilson
e) Catherine f) Gatsby

13 (possible answers)
- a) He keeps her locked in the house and decides to move West. He seems mad and desperate.
- b) First he is emotional and then he becomes serious and calm.

Page 92

14
- a) Tom says this to Nick after Daisy has

spoken to him at the beginning of the
- story. He is afraid of what Daisy might have told Nick.
- b) Nick says this to Gatsby at Gatsby's party because Nick has never met Gatsby.
- c) Gatsby says this to Nick about Wolfsheim when he is explaining how powerful he is.
- d) Gatsby says this to Nick because he wants to go for a drive and talk to him.
- e) George Wilson says this to Tom because he is desperate to move away.
- f) Daisy says this to Gatsby because he is trying to get her to say that she only loves him.

Page 95

20
- a) Gatsby tries to achieve the American Dream through money and success.
- b) Nick tries to become part of society.
- c) Jordan tries to win competitions and be present at as many functions as possible.
- d) Myrtle wants to leave her husband for Tom.

Page 97

23 a) under b) inside c) out d) off
e) to f) from g) over h) up i) in
j) on
24
- a) a mansion is a large luxurious house
- b) an apartment is a house on one floor inside a building with other apartments
- c) a palace is where a royal person lives
- d) a house is the general name for a place to live

Page 98

1 a) 1 b) 2 c) 2 d) 1
2 a) T b) T c) T d) F e) F f) T
g) F h) F i) T j) F k) F l) F m) F
n) T o) F p) F

國家圖書館出版品預行編目資料

大亨小傳 (The Great Gatsby) / F. Scott Fitzgerald
著；安卡斯 譯 . 一初版 . 一 [臺北市]：寂天文化，
2012.3　面；公分 .

中英對照
ISBN　978-986-184-976-8　(25K 平裝附光碟)
1. 英語　　2. 讀本

805.18　　　　　　　　　　101002439

■作者 _ F. Scott Fitzgerald　■改寫 _ David A. Hill　■譯者 _ 安卡斯
■主編 _ 黃鈺云　■製程管理 _ 黃敏昭　■文字校對 _ 李岳霞
■出版者 _ 寂天文化事業股份有限公司　■電話 _ 02-2365-9739　■傳真 _ 02-2365-9835
■網址 _ www.icosmos.com.tw　■讀者服務 _ onlineservice@icosmos.com.tw
■出版日期 _ 2012年3月 初版一刷（250101）
■郵撥帳號 _ 1998620-0 寂天文化事業股份有限公司
■訂購金額600（含）元以上郵資免費　■訂購金額600元以下者，請外加郵資60元
■若有破損，請寄回更換　■版權所有，請勿翻印